PECKHAM RYE

PECKHAM RYE

MILES PRINCE

Troubador Publishing Ltd
Unit E2 Airfield Business Park,
Harrison Road, Market Harborough,
Leicestershire LE16 7UL
Tel: 0116 279 2299
Email: books@troubador.co.uk
Web: www.troubador.co.uk

ISBN 9781836282235

British Library Cataloguing in Publication Data.
A catalogue record for this book is available from the British Library.

The manufacturer's authorised representative in the EU for product
safety is Authorised Rep Compliance Ltd, 71 Lower Baggot Street,
Dublin D02 P593 Ireland (www.arccompliance.com).

Printed and bound in Great Britain by 4edge Limited
Typeset in 12pt Garamond Pro by Troubador Publishing Ltd, Leicester, UK

For Walter Mosley, who sustained me over the decades.

To my parents, who created this story.

CONTENTS

INTRODUCTION

Joseph Wright, a young, alcoholic man of Afro-European heritage, lives alone in a Peckham council flat earning a living by taking risks and helping people in his community. A chance phone call leads him on a tense trail from the poverty of urban housing estates to gold mines in Ghana, and from the sinister underbelly of London's global service sector to the conspicuous riches of Mayfair.

As Joseph struggles to make sense of his own story, he takes the reader on a dangerous journey of discovery towards a truth that should be as unpalatable as it is unacceptable for those who still want to believe in democracy. In doing so, he finds both personal and institutional reasons for the gaping inequality in economic outcomes we see today and has to confront powerful forces, who, for hundreds of years, have captured much of the world's history for their own ends.

1

FRIDAY EVENING

It was a beautiful Four One Nine. Perfect. They contacted him out of the blue saying they'd set up an investment account in his name with two thousand pounds in it. Over the course of the next few weeks, they'd messaged daily providing good news about the performance of 'his' portfolio. And by the end, he must have wanted so much to believe he'd earned big from investments he'd had no hand in making. All that was left to do was transfer his life's meagre savings to bitcoin to cover their fees and walk off with twenty times that amount. Money for free. What luck in such a luckless world! So it had gone.

He had begun a kind of snivelling when I'd outlined my position on the matter. 'So what you want me to do? Fly to Lagos or Dubai or wherever the hell these people are and do what? Ask nicely for your money back? I can't help you. The weak end up getting taken by those who are strong, my friend. That's the way it has always been and always will be.'

The pleas became more of a whine, higher-pitched, panicking, like an infant abandoned on the train platform watching his parents glide serenely away.

I slammed off the call then, a slash of anger fizzing up in my body, bouncing off invisible knots of pain. Some people trudged to me tiredly, heaving the luggage of their futile lives and I tried to help, sifting through the stale garments, finding patterns and pathways to the surface.

But others drifted in on a cloud of plain fantasy! This deluded congregation were the time-wasters, the nonsense talkers, the denialists. They fancied that I was some miracle worker who could turn the bile of their confused existence into sweet flowing wine. The scam artists depended on clueless individuals such as these.

I reclined into my balcony chair, head shaking, eyes startled in disbelief at the stupidity. A finger of brandy lingered suggestively in the heavy crystal of its tumbler, eager to take the edge off. Marital effluent of the Forsters downstairs could often be heard spilling out in guttural shouting, but tonight there was only peace.

Who could tell? Maybe it was simply the phrase that had set me off: 'Four One Nine', that section of Nigeria's criminal code dealing with fraud. The humour it contained, dry as ancient bones, was deployed like a float vest to lighten the burden of the lives we were given. I'd heard it sung countless times over the years, a prayer to the torments of desperate anonymity.

But then the sniveller had somehow reminded me of my father too – that barrelled West African intonation, the stilted, almost formal use of English…

Across the road from where I sat, Peckham Rye loomed in the late-evening shadow, an impossibly large titan waiting to gain form and claim the world as its own. Old broken stories of men shuffled along the edge and people walked their dogs, some picking up the animals' leavings on the way, most not. There were kids too young to be out on their bikes, teenage lovers touching playfully and laughing loud.

The tide had subsided now, and, pressing deep into the cushion of my plastic seat, I remembered the counsellor I'd been sent to at fourteen before someone decided to give up and move on. There was the woman's blotchy, determined face, framed by straggly over dyed hair. Her small mouth asked me why I felt angry. *Joseph, can you imagine what might have triggered it?* She emphasised the word 'trigger' like I was some kind of loaded gun. So now I started imagining again, about the call I'd terminated, the voice of my father, and gnashing anger tore chaotically back in a torrent of words and feelings.

And what about me? Who saves me?!

The night wrapped itself confidently around the park, which spread out across the world. High up on the sixth floor, you could be an omnipotent proprietor of the dusk, controlling it solely with the power of imagination. The last injection of brandy was doing the trick, dulling feelings, searing those dripping raw-meat juices so they could be more easily swallowed. It was at this moment that my phone rang. I looked for the number: 'Uncle Ernest'.

I called him 'Uncle' but we weren't related. Ernest was a West African man in whose home I'd found sanctuary when things with my mum were on the slide. Theirs was the type of family life I secretly craved. Both parents worked long shifts, but you always had rice and stew in the pot and the warmth of adults involved faithfully in the serious business of raising their seed. Aged six, their son, Joshua Kwame, had been my closest friend.

"Hi, Uncle."

"Joseph." He said it with the apprehension of one uncertain who he might be dealing with anymore. A few people close enough knew what had happened during my mum's illness, though nobody'd ever asked.

"How's Aunty Sonia?"

"Good! And Rachel's just finished her finals at Manchester."

"Well done her! Law, wasn't it?"

"Yes. We will be going up there for her graduation this autumn."

"And how's my boy, JK?"

He paused, steeling himself to do what he had to. He wasn't used to dancing on the wrong side of the street. It must have been something important.

"Uncle, what's happened to Joshua?" I uttered the question calmly, as the do gooder therapist might have done.

"Oh nothing, nothing too bad yet… He's, uh, having some issues at work."

The silence that followed was intended to lead the fifty-five-year-old into the big bad woods where one of Britain's truly good men could breathe the same musty air as its less fruitful subjects.

"You know when he came out of university four years ago, he got a job in the City at that bank."

"Yeah, GBC, wasn't it?"

"Global Banking Corporation. One of the world's biggest, he tells me. Well, he's having some problems there now."

"Sorry to hear, Uncle. What can I do to help?"

"I know you do things, favours for people in return for…"

"Uncle, for you and yours there is no 'return for'. Whatever I can do is free… you know that." I meant it. Without those sweet evenings and the Sunday afternoons at his, God knows what a ten-year-old me would have done away from a home with a mother who just couldn't deal. I relaxed into the balcony throne, basking in the warm fantasy of myself as the subject of Uncle Ernest's pub-time banter: talked about in hushed, tighter-pitched tones by men two generations my senior. At twenty-six, I already possessed a resumé that made it so.

"We've noticed JK become very depressed and withdrawn. The boy was going to get his own flat near the office last year…"

He half chuckled with the sorrow.

"But he's ditched that. He spends evenings in his room, won't talk much to us… we are concerned, Jojo." He invoked the name he'd used for me as a child, but we both knew this was no child's conversation.

"I don't know if it's this for sure but Joshua has been having issues at work ever since he applied to become a fully-fledged trader."

"Trouble?"

"Yes… with some white colleagues."

Everything fell into its proper place.

"They are saying he's not right for the job, they are pressuring him to leave the team. They keep telling him he's not a good fit."

"I see."

"There's a head-of-desk man that's particularly gotten into it, I believe. He's issued JK with reprimands and official warnings for no real reason that I can fathom."

Uncle Ernest sounded so pained. It hurt to hear how some parents could suffer for their own.

"How can I help, Uncle?"

"His name's Barker, Wade Barker – the desk head. I thought maybe… maybe…"

I left it hanging for a while. I may not have made it close to a university nor bagged a high-flying job at some fancy bank, but this man still came to me to save a son who had done all those things. His boy had learnt what the system wanted him to know but not what he needed to. Uncle Ernest understood this, just as he knew that where I came from fitted the problem as tightly as a Versace T-shirt.

"How about I check on Mr Barker, then, um… maybe have a small chat with him – just so he sets the record straight for our boy?" Jojo was gone. I was talking to my uncle, man to man. His need had sought out my skillset and it felt intoxicating. There was a pause at the other end as he thought things through: *a last chance to get out of this!* My mobile beeped in alarm. I let the second caller go.

"OK, that sounds like a plan, Joseph."

"I'll be in touch within a week."

Ernest didn't thank me before disconnecting. He was regretting it too much already. I leant into the problem, starting to play about with a few angles I might take with the head trader, Wade Barker. These finance guys all possessed deep fault lines, which is what pushed them to money ahead of everything else. And this was the part I enjoyed most about my chosen vocation: working people out, picturing what they might do and how to get to them. It was called empathy by some.

Night-time finished covering day with its death shawl. A couple more shots from the bottle imparted that loose feeling, which took the weight off the loneliness but wouldn't get rid of it altogether without quite a few more. I dialled Yiolanda.

"Hey, wassup, it's Jo."

"Joseph?" She was vaguely surprised to hear my voice.

"I was just thinking. About how it's so hard for a talented young black woman to really make it in the corporate world of this Britain today. I am surprised more don't run their own game – like you, I mean."

Yiolanda wasn't expecting this either, but if you are comfortable being yourself, very little can throw you.

"It isn't easy, Jo."

"I know. How was your day?"

"Not great. Had a problem with one of my belt suppliers, and I can't get hold of the right sauce for the fiftieth I'm doing next Saturday. But hey, these things are sent to test us."

"Maybe we should go for coffee soon – it would be good to see ya."

"Sure. I'm pretty busy but if you can come to the shop around eight."

After five years grafting, Yiolanda had expanded from a stall in Spitalfields Market to a retail unit on its west side, near Brick Lane. It sold fully priced clothes she called Flava Chic to the more adventurous woman working a hundred metres away in the financial district of the City of London. She also maintained a tidy second business on the side arranging catering events for a well-off West African clientele. These were people who were prepared to pay for the genuine taste of their favourite places from back home, served with the efficiency of an American fast food chain.

We had been at school together and some people were tethered by invisible ropes of destiny, but we both knew Yiolanda's poise wouldn't allow itself to sit next to such extreme imbalance for very long.

"I'll send you a text next week before I come."

The conversation helped but the loneliness gloomed its way back, surrounding me like the walls of some deep cave out of which there was no escape. I drank a few more, in the end shouting vulgar obscenities out at the world from my tiny balcony; expletives of pain and release. It wasn't the stabbing anger of my daytimes, more the cry of someone left for dead in the desert a thousand miles away from the nearest pool of water. After a while, I stumbled back into the living room and fell asleep on the couch that my father had bought with bad credit twenty years earlier.

2

SATURDAY

The call I'd missed, speaking to Uncle Ernest, had gone to voicemail. Listening to the message invited stabs of adrenaline into a hungover body, which was quickly recovering with that magic potion known as youth. The caller not only had my number but knew my full name and said it with a Nigerian accent. My chimp brain wanted to call him back immediately, but the more evolved survivor kept it in check, let me plan for the bad things before engaging.

Orange juice, two bananas, then a shower completed the restoration that youth had mostly already forged. I donned the morning's uniform; deliberately unmemorable. Then running shoes; dark with no detailing. The slim path through British justice that was 'reasonable doubt' became a valley when describing a young brown Londoner dressed this way. I decided to bypass the lift – someone had pissed in it and running down six flights would warm up my legs for the weekly jog to the Saturday Service.

Bursting across the road and into the park, I planned out a useful circuit. Then respiring towards that aerobic trance to which every runner is addicted, my mind veered elsewhere, sifting through the foliage of memory's elusive tree.

By thirteen, life had gone badly. My mother's reaction to abandonment by 'the Nigerian', as she ended up calling him, led her to a mix of antidepressants and booze, which were taking their toll after five years. I got into a lot of fights at school, mostly still childish rehearsals of the anger that the combatants were struggling to contain, but after one beating too many, I realised that success in violence needed to be taught.

Some weeks later, I'd joined Poorang's group of loose ends looking for a middle. And Poorang was that centre: a ponytailed fighting trainer who gave Thursday lessons in a rented church hall and on Saturday mornings, in and around his block of flats – the Saturday Service. I'd seen him twice a week for twelve years but knew only a few details from the life of the stout, long-haired Iranian immigrant, even though his teaching had saved me great harm on more than one occasion.

When I'd dared to knock on his front door, Poorang had taken both sides of my face with strong palms, looking into the young teenager's eyes like an optometrist for the soul. "OK, I'll start you off on a pound a session. We do Saturdays by the garages down there. It's got cover if it rains."

I later felt, with that look, he was gauging what the adult-to-be might do with the gifts he would endow. As the pupil had gotten older, his reservations about this one had grown.

I sped up a touch, drifting past a fit woman in nice-fitting leggings, and then returned to the whispers of intuition that linked past and present. Poorang's scheme of violence was focused on the one thing: survival. Those lessons would be needed soon as we careered towards adulthood like driverless trucks on a nighttime motorway. Plenty had been learnt from the ponytailed missionary, but Poorang's first mantra, the thing with which he started every session, had always proved the most useful: 'Don't get caught!'. That sometimes meant you needed to be fitter than the next man, who would usually tire after a two hundred-metre sprint because he'd not trained hard enough. In most ways that mattered, 'Don't get caught' had formed the founding principle for whatever you called what I did.

My mobile vibrated in agitation. It was the same number that had left the voicemail. I picked up, sitting on a bench that would otherwise have passed me by. The fit jogger soon came back to me and I watched her disappear gracefully into the greenery. Then there it was again. The speaker had that voice – the boom of an older West African man – another proxy for a father I'd only known for a third of my existence.

"Hello, is this Joseph Wright?"

I let him hang a few seconds.

"How did you get my number?"

He had some notion of why I had asked. The sort of person he wanted surely would.

"Remy. Remy Hammond from the church. She knew your father. She told me she had dealings with you a couple of years ago."

Dealings. Remy had trouble with her second marriage. Maybe she'd been seeing other men, maybe not, but her husband became convinced of the fact and started turning these speculations into slaps and punches. She went to the elders of her church for help: men of similar age and background to her husband. The rumours had already spread. Desperate to avoid ending up nursing some serious injuries, Remy had approached the head of the Ghanaian family in the UK of which she was a proud member. But he was a man more equipped to drink himself to a stupor at weekends than offer wise marriage counsel. He'd told her to go back to her man and try much harder. Finally at the end of her wits, after another violent night-time encounter, a younger church evangelist reminded her that she still had one card left to play in the game of marriage survival, which was me.

After some checks, I had gone to see the man at his house, sat down at his small dining table as if I owned the place and persuaded him of the two options available. The first was he keep his shit in check with Mrs Hammond. The second was he leave if he knew deep down he couldn't do this because if he touched her again, he would suffer great injury at my hand. Within two days, he'd moved out. Remy never forgave me for the loss of her marriage. All she'd wanted, it seemed, was her husband minus the fist.

"I see. How can I help you, Mr…"

"Folarin. Tunde Folarin. I really need to explain face to face. I am on nights this month. Can we meet later today somewhere, before work?" His eagerness made him less nervous than they usually were, which set off an amber light somewhere.

"Where do you live?"

"Lewisham."

"Alright – there's that big park in Lewisham at… umm…"

"Ladywell?"

"Yes. I'll meet you by the entrance nearest the station."

"There are a few stations around that place."

He knew the area where he claimed to live.

"The station that is named for the park. 2pm."

"Fine. How will I know you?"

"You won't. But I will know you because you are going to send me a picture of yourself."

It wasn't a request. I was not interested in meeting a friend of a woman with a score to settle, without having the type of advantages that kept a person breathing. It could have been Remy's violent husband planning some crazy revenge for the humiliation I'd inflicted. She might even have been helping him. I jumped off the bench and sprinted towards Poorang's garages. It was a quarter to ten. I was nearly late and I detested lateness.

If you watch Floyd Mayweather's fights, it is apparent that, by instinct, he usually can sense what the opponent is going to throw before it happens. Poorang had brought his battered laptop to the Saturday Service to ask us how that might be. We huddled around the device as our teacher showed us how decades of repetition from an early age enabled Mayweather to instinctively understand what was and wasn't mechanically viable for a body in a certain position. He knew which types of hard punches were possible given the positioning of an opponent's feet, the angle of their limbs, the torque implicit in their waist and shoulders. He could, therefore, usually avoid what was coming and, more important still, punish the assailant with his own blows just after they'd pulled their failed trigger. Most of his victims either stopped trying halfway through or gassed out under the mental stress of fighting someone always that step ahead.

Showering at home, I ran through how I would

get to Ladywell two hours early, hiking up from the southern arena end equipped with binoculars. There was a nice position on the park's eastern greenery where those heading in from the train station could be monitored. I had picked Ladywell for this vantage point and because of its open spaces, offering plenty of time to run then vanish into trees or concrete.

The caution wasn't needed this time. At 1:45pm, a bald-headed, middle-aged West African approached from Ladywell station. He stopped at the entrance to the park and waited, mopping the sweat of anxiety with a grey handkerchief. I called, he picked up and we met at a bench ten minutes' walk inside.

The first thing that distinguished the man was the way he carried a tall frame. His wasn't the beaten-down bearing of some first-generation immigrants who'd come to me: people who life had forced to swap poverty where they'd started for the bottom of the pile, where they'd ended up. Folarin's back remained straight; he walked steadily and precisely as if the space he occupied was as valid as anyone else's. This man had been something back home, still felt he was someone, in fact. He looked me directly in the eye as he pulled up to sit.

Then there was the way he spoke.

"Mr Wright, I presume," he said to the brown-skinned, blue hoodie-wearing youth who stood before him. I was probably at least ten years younger than he wanted but he wasn't thrown.

"Joseph."

"Tunde." He nodded, focussing past me at the bench. Scared people were on such high alert they usually couldn't give up anything much beyond their fear, so I gave it time to dissolve a touch.

"So why are we here, Tunde?"

"I work as a security guard at a big law firm, Cubbins, Jacques and Heward. Sometimes days, sometimes nights."

"An interesting job for someone with your qualifications... and your experience."

The man appreciated that I understood but wasn't here to tell his own sorry tale. I was impressed by the commitment to whatever cause had made him dial my number.

"I have a friend there, also part of security, a Ghanaian, Yaw Asante. Yaw means 'Thursday-born' according to those Ghanaian day names. He's disappeared for two weeks. I've been to his flat, but there's no sign of him." The Nigerian rummaged in the pockets of the ill-fitting uniform he now had to wear, eventually producing two keys.

"Is he a good friend?"

The older man jerked with indignation, but he had phoned me and I didn't have to wait long for his composure to return.

"Yaw came from Ghana thirty years ago. He was high up in the police there, investigating corruption. His investigations got a bit close to... let's say, powerful government officials. He had to leave fast, got to the UK through Cote d'Ivoire somehow."

"So you think old enemies followed him here?"

"I doubt those fools have the resources or the will. The ones he was investigating are old men now or dead. But who knows? My first thought was he'd been deported by British Immigration Services, but he assured me his papers here were fine."

"I see. Why are you taking the risk of meeting someone like me? He must be a very good friend." Folarin was easily smart enough to cope with the disrespect of directness. I had to ask because I'd never been in a situation where some idea of why people were doing what they were doing didn't lower risk.

His eyes showed momentary resistance until the considerable intellect took back control. He sighed deeply.

"His story and mine aren't so different. Different country, thirty years separating them but not so different. Only Yaw really has any idea of what has happened to me in the last six months. He helped me, put me up on his sofa when I needed. I haven't known him that long, but he was like a brother in many ways."

"You were important back in Nigeria?"

Tunde Folarin aged a decade in front of me, but still managed to look both sad and defiant at the same time.

"Head of a department at the Central Bank, before…" I gazed absently at a cluster of thriving trees, a stare with less feeling than if I was waiting at the counter for a hamburger. The economist struggled to distil the mess of life for his indifferent listener.

"In December 2013, Central Bank Governor Sanusi wrote a letter, which was leaked to the Nigerian press, asking President Goodluck Jonathan where billions of dollars of our oil revenues had gone. He was quickly dismissed."

"And some of you were felt to be too closely affiliated to him?"

"Sanusi tried to change things. He was from a powerful family, so he was able to try. But those of us without that type of backing…"

"So, it was time to leave the country."

Folarin remained proud but the effect of the last six months was etched into every hopeless gesture.

"Your family?"

"My children are grown up. They and my wife are still in Nigeria. It's been very hard for them. I am waiting for a year or two to see what the options are. I fund them with what I earn here. I can't get permanent citizenship for five years so this is the work I do."

I gave a pause for the man's feelings to pull back again texting him an email address I used. After a while, I could see it was time to try and extract more.

"Yaw Asante attended church?"

"The Holy Spirit Revealed. It is somewhere in Croydon. Church was never really my cup of tea, but I go to one near here now to be with my people. A man in my situation needs that."

"Can you email me what you have on Asante: address, mobile numbers, any friends or family? I assume you all work for an agency?"

He nodded acceptance.

"How much will you charge? I don't have a lot."

"Let's see what it costs," I said to the poor central banker, "but I won't go over a thousand without calling you. I'll take those keys now too."

Folarin passed them without thought, swiftly, as you would to shed a load that you have no way of carrying.

"There's one more thing. I forgot but it's just been coming back to me as you said the word 'friend' earlier. Yaw had become very good friends with one of the lawyers at the firm where we work, an English man. You know, some of them like to think they really love Africa. Yaw had told him his story and the man was helping him somehow. I saw them together quite a bit at lunchtimes. They met for supper after work and, he said, at weekends too."

It was funny how often the most important things got lost until the end. I waited neutrally for his brain to manifest more.

"His name is Michaels, Lawrence Michaels. He was advising Yaw on some land issue in Ghana from the little he told me. I have not seen Michaels for over a week either. I asked someone at the firm and they said he was on compassionate leave. His mother has died."

left some messages, then called Kate, who, depending on the day, might have said she was my girlfriend. Kate worked for a busy estate agent that was riding the wave of local improvement. A higher class of person without the wallet to necessarily satisfy their self-image had been buying into parts of South London for quite some time. Kate was hoping to work her way from the servitude of administrative assistant to the exhilarations of a sales role. The woman was determined to improve her lot and I got the feeling she'd be off and away from me once that promotion came in.

"How's my favourite detective today?" she said, failing to sell me the idea that she both admired what I did or was truly interested in it.

"Got a few balls in the air all of a sudden."

Had she not been at work, Kate might have wanted to talk more about my balls being in the air but her game voice was firmly on at the moment.

"Not sure when I'm gonna be free this week."

There was no disappointment in her, merely a logistical note in the diary, something akin to *take the cat to the vet* or *nail appointment with Vera*.

"Oh, that's a pity. OK, babe, call me when you know more. I've gotta go."

Kate sometimes decided to turn up at my flat unannounced, early on in our relationship wearing very little under her coat, but more lately to check if I was cheating on her. I badly needed to keep this woman safe and away from the flat. It didn't cost much in terms of time and was necessary because there was a problem somewhere in Folarin's story.

The school counsellor had once broken down the term hypervigilance to me. It's what happens when, for example, a baby grows up in a household where physical or emotional violence make up the standard diet. Day by day, the child victim's body becomes accustomed to always being on alert, ready to run or fight. It learns to look for small signs of impending danger that subtle changes of mood or volume might convey. As it grows, the child will come up with all kinds of shit to avoid the various catastrophic scenarios of annihilation that its mind has been conditioned to expect. I knew at the time she'd meant me, but a Ghanaian security guard had disappeared and the mother of an English lawyer trying to help him had died.

3

SUNDAY

I counted at least a dozen religious establishments in Croydon. The taxi dropped me on a main artery, and I walked the few streets back, noting various possible escape routes along the way. The Holy Spirit Revealed was a spacious but basic box of a building, which might even have been partly built of plywood above head height, such was the focus on cost. A small, unpainted cross hung precariously over the front entrance.

I quickly caught the eyes of a few people standing outside, checking messages and chatting – enough to gain access without anyone asking, but not so much that they would get a long look. I was sporting a cloth cap and fake spectacles. It had felt appropriate to be wearing smart black trousers, a cream-white shirt tucked neatly in, brown belt, gold-buckle but still black trainers in case quick getaway on foot was needed. Beyond the cross, there was a covered vestibule, where you could hang back to watch what was occurring inside through the wired glass of the main hall door.

It was 2pm, so the festivities were in full swing. In the left corner of the large room, there sat a four-piece band producing a song, which gave the impression of being able to keep going for hours if need be. Half the congregation was up and dancing, others nodded in personal musical mediations. After a few minutes, the master of ceremonies and pastor stood to address everyone, welcoming new entrants, saying a couple more things about why they were all there, then got off the makeshift stand to let the music flow. I was pleasantly surprised by his brevity, having more than once had to listen to lengthy streams of consciousness from older West African priests who weren't wise enough to care that they didn't know.

A new tune lit up, and the religious discotheque revved into full gear. In time, the lead guitarist put down his instrument and danced over to mingle, which, if anything, encouraged the remaining bass, drums and synth to inject more pace. Responding to their efforts, another parishioner picked it up and started to extract his own truth from the electrically animated strings.

There was a small café open, thirty metres down and across the street, to which I quietly retreated. I sat with my back to the proprietor, ordered continuous coffee, orange juice, a slow omelette lunch. Then, as the afternoon petered out, stale apple pie served with overly sweet ice cream. At around 5pm, an exodus of rejuvenated people poured from the double doors, relieved of burdens and ready for another week in the battle that was Britain.

After the crowd had scattered away to their lives, I sauntered into the hall where three church people were still cleaning up. One of them, a self-appointed bouncer, approached. He was ageing but built from the ground up and had been very strong at one time.

"What can we do for you, brother? Hey, is that… Joseph?"

It was irritating to be uncovered so easily.

"I knew you when you were a boy at school. How's your father? Oh, I forgot. He's back home in Nigeria now. Yes."

A shadow of violence puckered my shoulders.

"Ashley Adebayo. I'm his father!"

I nodded, relaxing only a touch. Ashley had told me some pretty bad things about his home life over the years.

"Oh, Ashley. How's he doing? I've not seen him for six months I reckon."

The man's arms slumped by his side.

"He's fallen in with some people. I don't like them at all. I pray for him here every Sunday, Joseph."

I knew this already because I knew the people Ashley moved with. They were the type even I avoided unless I really needed something.

"Oh, sorry to hear that, Mr Adebayo. It's hard out there, you know – for boys like us."

"Yes, that's what you kids always seem to say, Joseph, but I cannot understand it; this language you all use. Who are these 'boys like us'? Boys with no plan? No desire to do better? And tell me why, when he have worked so hard to give you the chances we never had?"

The older man's sadness was transforming now into something like anger. I watched it happening, wondering how many beatings the shape-shifting had meant for my friend when he was younger.

"What about you? I heard you were getting into trouble too, Joseph?"

"Guess you'll have to pray for me as well, Mr Adebayo. I need saving more than most."

Had he cared to pay attention, the big church warden would have spotted that my eyes gazed at him now with a predatory calm. I was getting more ready, calculating what he might be able to do, given the geometry his legs formed with the floor. I had subtly shifted sideways, enough to allow me to pivot out of the way of his lead left hand if he tried to grab.

But the man was carried by glaciers of emotion so tall they were curtailing his ability to fashion this sort of arithmetic. He came on stronger, and I floated back a touch more now, very aware of the positions of the two other parishioners. They'd not be able to get to me by the time Adebayo Senior lay injured on the floor.

"I just don't know what is wrong with your

generation. Ashley used to say you were the cleverest in the year – in the whole school even – but look at you! What have you achieved in life, Joseph? Tell me – what?"

On the first *'what?'*, the gesticulating bully took an exasperated step towards me. I said nothing, removed the fake spectacles and started delicately flexing my hands. Then, right there on the precipice, he stopped, waking from his bad nightmare just before the screaming fall. The brute withdrew quickly, stumbling backwards, tangling his legs on an unstacked chair. Then, part bent at the waist trying to recover his balance, a confused Dr Jekyll scrambled back into view, rescuing its Nigerian Mr Hyde.

"Why are you here, Joseph?"

The pastor was in the toilet for a long time. I waited for him in a small utility room at the back of the hall, shaking off lingering filaments of violence, casually scouring the drab walls and desk for any information. This closet room was all business: bills, ledgers, lists of names and a tall metal office chest of drawers standing on guard in the corner. He paused a moment by the door before entering and I rose to meet the short barrel-stomached man who carried a remarkable mirth in his calculating eyes.

"How can I help you, Joseph?" He'd been briefed on his way in by the Nigerian.

"Hello, Mr…"

"Daniels. Pastor Ekow Daniels," he pronounced with relish.

"I enjoyed the service. I like the way you just let it flow."

Daniels looked up at me with a millisecond's impatience. He wanted to know my business here. An instant later, the laughing eyes returned to their job of convincing anyone and everyone that they were bursting with love.

"Yes, we believe that being joyful is God's work and that spreading that joy is the church's role. The Holy Spirit is for all men and all women."

"I am looking for one of your congregation, Yaw Asante. He seems to have disappeared."

God's messenger shifted just slightly in his seat – he didn't know about the disappearance, but he knew about something.

"I see. That sounds worrying. Maybe we should call the police?"

And he wasn't going to tell me.

"Yes, worth a try but I doubt he'll be anywhere near top of their list if you do. In the meantime, was he worried about anything in the last few weeks? It has been suggested that he was involved in some new business dealings. In Ghana maybe."

The priest had a tell, an eyebrow that levitated

when something he was trying to hide, hit the bullseye of his truth.

"No... not as far as I could say. He was uh... a very private man."

"You know about his history, the troubles back in Ghana?"

"Yes. Stories. There are so many stories from our generation. The things people went through then."

"Maybe a former police chief wanted a way back in. Back to Ghana, to his old life. Better than working security here I imagine."

The eyebrow shot up and below it the eyes calculated briefly before quickly assuming their dance of priestly love.

"I really do not know, Joseph. People don't always tell their pastors the... the difficult stuff. You know what I mean?"

I decided to break in later to have a better look through the desk and that filing cabinet now directly behind Daniels' muscular shoulders.

"I guess the devil takes all the bad, which leaves only the good for Jesus."

He smiled, more in relief than anything else.

"Thanks for your time, Pastor. If he contacts you, can you text me here? People are really worried about him."

The man saw me to the church door, eyes simply bursting with mirth. Adebayo had gone, but outside, twenty metres from the building, one of the two younger men who'd been putting chairs away approached. He was lanky, my age and carried a seriousness about him, like some academics or writers do.

"Samuel Quartey."

"Alright, Samuel, shall we go for a walk?"

Samuel shot a worried glance back at the crucifix.

"I like the way this church does things. You been coming here long?"

The lanky academic was calming down quickly the further away we got.

"Most of my life. I came to Jesus through the music really."

"Someone once said music is the mathematics of the soul. If so, God must be a composer."

The man at my side shot me a quizzical look. The balmy evening carried us along on a tour of the backstreets of Croydon.

"Pastor Daniels is interesting – he laughs with his eyes."

"Yes. He built this church from nothing over thirty years. We have a thousand regulars now. He's different to most. Doesn't judge or tell us all what to do."

"He get involved with the lives of his flock?"

"Yes, sometimes, when they need help. People fall and it's not easy to get back up again."

"Tell me about it, bro. What do you do, Samuel?"

"I am training to be a psychiatrist."

"So you're a doctor already?"

"Yes."

"Why psychiatry?"

"I've always been interested in the mystery of mind. It's kind of religious itself when you start really considering it. That composer God's greatest tune maybe. Plus, with so many of our people in need of help, there aren't many black psychiatrists out there practising."

"True. My mum's white but she's in the Maudsley at the moment."

"How long?"

"Nearly ten years on and off. She finds it difficult out here now."

I felt the sympathy in the look he offered. He understood what it might have meant for me.

"Your parents are both Ghanaian, though, right?"

"Yep. They are looking to retire soon and go back there to live."

"Do you know Yaw Asante?" The question had hovered in the background for a while and he was more than ready.

"Uncle Yaw. He is an interesting man. Very smart yet compassionate too. He somehow understands what makes people tick."

"How so?"

"He's one of those people. They could go anywhere and strike up a conversation with a stranger. And when you talk to him, you like him straight off the bat."

"He's gone missing and a good friend of his hired me to find out why. Has he been into anything the last few weeks, with Pastor Daniels maybe?"

"Not sure but they've been talking a lot in the back office after church service on Sundays. I've heard them speak about some issue back in Ghana – when I'm putting the chairs away, you know."

The eavesdropping psychiatrist was almost too good to be true.

"Why are you helping me, Samuel?"

"I saw you with Adebayo. He's a bully. Does it with everyone one way or another. I saw that you understood this immediately. You would have followed through with him and he realised. I guess I admire people who stand up to bullies. I really like Yaw too. He's a kind of father figure to me in a way my own cannot be. He possesses what you might call genuine empathy."

"Here's my phone number in case you think of anything else. I am sure there's more than a lot I could learn from you, Samuel."

Quartey breathed in deeply, acknowledging in my words the lonely road that explorers of the soul had to travel.

The Holy Spirt Revealed had a security budget set somewhere near zero. It was easy to jump over the gate that led into the thick weeds of its rear garden. The rickety wooden door was almost inviting someone to smash through, but I took longer, picking the lock, not wanting the priest to suspect I'd returned .

The utility room wasn't blessed with any protection at all. I carefully sifted through the filing cabinet looking for outliers, things that had nothing to do with church business but might have everything to do with a man's disappearance. The place was as silent as a mortuary. After half an hour I came across some photocopies of title documents from a Ghanaian land registry. The property seemed to be held in the name of an entity called R.A. Capital. I took pictures, then arranged all as I'd found it before stealing away like the thief in the night that I actually was.

4

MONDAY MORNING

South London felt tight the next morning, as if stifling summer humidity laced with the excretions of a million vehicles were certain to shorten life. Colourfully attired joggers dotted Peckham Rye, ploughing faithfully through the substandard air on their way to the fitness heavens of which they dreamt. I dialled the next step.

"Joseph?"

Everett Langston ran and owned one of London's biggest employment agencies, placing cleaners, janitors and catering staff into the thousands of businesses that needed them across the capital. A tall, unassuming-looking man, who wouldn't spend a hundred pounds on a jacket, he was possibly the UK's most successful home-grown black entrepreneur. He kept a low profile but was a legend in his chosen game.

Everett had called me three years earlier to access a capacity for lying and manipulation that would deliver answers. He was concerned that the profit from a part of his empire seemed to be larger than it should be. Here was a businessperson so devoted to the longevity of his operation that he was worried about making too much money! I liked him immediately. I went in, working on various evening shifts, and, after a few weeks, uncovered some interesting facts.

Langston's right-hand man, who was paid a share of profit, had recruited a few extra services to the company's portfolio. Some of the firm's cleaners were being used to courier cocaine, hidden in the heels of their shoes, to monied addicts, working in the law firms of Holborn. The right-hand man was putting it all through the company, effectively laundering the proceeds at the same time. Had I not found this out for him, Everett's business would, at some point, have been destroyed and he would certainly have faced a long stretch in jail. He owed me and that was convenient.

"Hey, Everett – how's tings?"

"Busy as always, JJ. Busy. What can I do for you?"

Over the years, we were developing quite a relationship. I had become his alter ego somehow, a shadow-Everett, whose existence allowed him to carry on out there in the daytime glare of corporate success. This also meant that he saw me as an equal, and I was guessing Everett Langston didn't have many of those.

"You do the cleaning for Cubbins, Jacques and Heward?"

"Yes. Won the contract off Brightling in 2010. You need to get in there?"

Everett knew I wouldn't do anything to mess up a relationship with a client for him unless I really had no choice. He also liked the idea of me getting back inside his operation from time to time.

"Can you put me on the third floor for the 6.30pm shift tonight?"

"Done."

"How many in the crew? Any familiar faces?"

When working for Everett's firm, I went by the name Chris Brown, a back-handed tribute to the R&B singer. I didn't like the sound of the man, but then most didn't like the sound of me and nobody ever asked why.

Yaw Asante lived walking distance from one of the world's leading financial centres, but his small dwelling should have been situated in a different country altogether. The housing estate had been built between the wars by people who would never have to live in the stifling dens they bequeathed others. The buildings themselves had long ago fallen into a quiet disrepair. Those who suffered living there had little choice but to stay and no way to make it better.

The single lock of the front door would have been

easy to manipulate but gave instantly to the keys Tunde Folarin had supplied. It opened timidly onto a small living room-cum-kitchenette whose fifteen-square metres formed the major part of the affair. Asante may not have been a tidy man but living alone all these years had almost made it so. There were photos on every piece of the peeling wall – black and whites of Accra dwellers, dressed in clothes of the 1970s and '80s. A brightly coloured print of a blond, blue-eyed Jesus promised to save all who came to him. Above the duel-barred electric heater he used to survive the winter hung a gold-framed image of a woman with two young children. His Ghanaian family from way back when.

Asante had fallen asleep on his real life in Accra and was patiently waiting to wake up from the bad dream that was England. Apart from the gilt photo frames, everything inside was of the cheapest variety available from a patched-up mock-leather sofa, electronics brands I'd only barely heard of to the thin mattress he'd used for a bed.

I went through the place with slow precision, confident nobody would be interrupting. His one plastic file carried more pictures of those back home and back in time and decades-old correspondence from the woman who had been his wife thanking him for sending money. A few months earlier, he'd received the bad news about her, outlined in the cold medical language of a death certificate.

An ageing King James bible was stashed under the

mattress at the pillow end. Inside the cover, a fading message, *To my dear friend Yaw, may God strengthen you through all the trials that life brings – Ekow.* The pastor had simply been lying to protect an old friend. Beyond this, Yaw Asante didn't have much at all: no diary, no phone book or bank records, no recordings on the old voice machine he kept alongside the landline. A man was gone. The already faint footprint he'd left on a Britain where he didn't want to be had dissolved completely.

The flat sat adjacent to the building's stairs, so was neighboured on only one side. I knocked on the flaked paint of the next door until someone came to the square frosted glass panel in it and shouted angrily through.

"Yes, what do you want?"

"I am a private detective and have been retained by the estate of a wealthy West African businessman to find your neighbour, Mr Yaw Asante."

"He keeps to hisself. I don't know where he is so why don't you piss off!"

I made a clearing sound with my throat.

"That's a pity… because Mr Asante has been named as a beneficiary in the dead businessman's will. The estate also has given me a mandate to pay those who help find its beneficiaries… If I could just come in for five minutes of your time, you might well be put up for some of that reward."

The anger subsided on the other side of the glass square and was balancing the risk of letting someone in against the possibility of the cash on offer. Suddenly, the door gaped open and there stood a gaunt seventy-year-old man whose unwashed, grey vest matched the rest of him. A small mongrel of some sort whimpered around his yellowing toenails.

"You'd better come in then," he said almost hospitably through a flash of decaying teeth.

While Yaw Asante half existed in a setting of disciplined nothingness, his neighbour lived in the bosom of dereliction. I made my way into the narrow corridor and could see that the dog didn't get out much because its hardened turds sat like monuments to mental illness every foot or so. I followed the man down his hallway. Glancing left, I noticed he kept piles of rubbish where he should have bathed. He moved jerkily, head ducking under fear of shame or judgement or just out of habit in a world that had dealt him such a badly losing hand. I maneuvered myself around the dog's leavings while my host was more than happy to kick them along the carpet on his way. We arrived at a tiny dark living room and he actually plumped up a cushion on the filthy sofa before gesturing at it for me to sit. The dog muzzled around my feet excitedly. It might not have seen another soul in here for years. The master of the house looked at me greedily.

"So what's all this about a reward then?"

"You are Mr...?"

"Castle."

"Well, Mr Castle, the rich man's estate is paying out

significant amounts of money and wants to find those who've been nominated. If you knew where he went or, um, had some idea who with, I am certain Mr Asante would appreciate the favour you'd done him too. As well as the reward, I mean."

The eyes bulged slightly, making their owner look more skull-like – finally his ship had arrived. I realised then that Castle was much closer to forty than seventy. He hadn't even asked for my name or ID; such was the desperation that blossomed where he sat.

"I don't know where he went but I saw him leave with three men two Mondays back. I was on the way from the job centre. Argh! Getting a job nowadays – no-one's hiring! But they go on and on at us like we aren't trying or nuthin'." The smell of the man wafted towards me, weaving its own tale about the impossibility of finding gainful employment.

"Three men. Did you see their faces?"

"Yeah, they were white. Big fuckers too like… like proper rugby players, you know – not yer pansy footballers. Those cunts get paid a fucking fortune to fall over every time someone touches 'em."

He'd probably not spoken to anyone for a while, so I nodded in agreement but didn't want to stay there any longer than was necessary.

"Did you notice anything else about them?"

"Not really. I was quite far away but I saw 'em all, alright. They had a nice motor – a dark-green Benz. Nearly new. A big saloon. He got in and it sped off."

"OK, thanks, Mr… Mr?"

"Castle. I told you that already! What about this money then?"

I took out a ten-pound note and handed it over.

"Let's call this an advance. I'll be back once we've found Mr Asante."

He examined the paper hungrily. The Queen's head smiled mysteriously back at him opposite the orangish-brown engraver's work. Castle was pleased with the morning's endeavour.

"Alright, alright, thank you. I'm here mostly so see you next time."

The dog yapped behind me as I navigated the hallway's assault course and burst out of the door back into sanity. I hadn't had to give a penny but felt something in there with him, an echo of a possible future. That ten-pound note was a down payment on buying a different one.

5

MONDAY AFTERNOON

Haggerston to Denmark Hill wasn't a long journey by train but it gave enough time to chew over the most difficult aspects of things as they stood. Those men in the green Mercedes represented an escalating likelihood of violence in pursuing the Ghanaian's disappearance. It was time to recruit help. I pondered the curse of bad fathers, dialling my old school friend.

"Adebayo!"

"Hey, Joseph – long time, bruv!" Despite the environment of regular brutality in which he'd been marinaded, Ashley's voice still held that childlike wonder at the mystery of it all.

"I saw your pops yesterday at his church."

"That man! I don't deal with him anymore, bruv – you know how it is – Nigerian parents always on your case for one reason or another."

"Yeah I hear it. What you doin' now? You were working with Cushnie last time we spoke."

The pause at the end of my question told me quite a few things. Ashley had been both a seller and consumer of class A drugs since he'd escaped our school at sixteen. It was possible that addiction had taken away his viability and I needed to see him to check how far he'd travelled down that line.

"Listen, maybe we could meet up later. Got a thing to run by you. I am working on a job in Holborn – could meet at that park round the back about 9pm… Ashley?"

"OK, bro! I'll see you there." I sensed an apprehension in him but couldn't tell if it was wariness of me or a lack of confidence that he was good for anything anymore.

"Behind the tennis courts. The building in the middle."

Across the road from Denmark Hill station was a hospital tasked with treating mental illness on behalf of the wider consensus of what was sane. I arrived promptly for visiting, passed warily though the entrance, then was buzzed in beyond reception to the unit housing longer-stay female occupants. She was brought to the door of the brightly decorated room by two strong-looking men. Then she shuffled in, a short, fat, brown-haired woman who'd long ago lost any sense of taking care of herself. Today, she looked a touch less drugged than usual.

"Awright, Mum."

"Jo."

She generally had little to say to me and if she did, drifted off in a fog of confused internal stories about her own life and that of my father. So, for thirty minutes or so, I would sit and look at her, trying to figure out what the hell was going on in that mangled head. If we are the tales we tell ourselves, there were only desperate tragedies here. By the end, I often got so annoyed that I simply had to ask something.

"What if it's nothing good, Mum?"

"What?"

"I always wonder, what if there's fuck all going on inside your head when I visit except bitterness? What if you've not experienced a single decent thought while I've been here or won't for the rest of the day after I leave?"

She looked up. The drugs had robbed her of the old talent for explosive anger but the newer version of it, dressed in medicinally enforced calm, could cut as deeply.

"You don't have to come."

"No, I guess not. In truth, I don't know why I do."

Her eyes carried the blunt intensity of a hatred, initially reserved for my father and which, before she'd come here, had extended itself to all men of Nigerian origin, including me.

"Goodbye, Mum. See you next time."

I nodded to the tired desk nurse on the way out. They'd go now and scoop her back into whatever chair she was wedded to for the rest of the day. I was angry with myself. In spite of a weight of evidence curated over twenty-six years, I still yearned for more. She hadn't warranted the title of parent for well over a decade now. When would this stupid boy learn?

The losses of childhood flooded back in their various nondescript ways. I punched the number of someone whose childhood I knew had undoubtedly been worse than mine. I didn't want to call him, but it was that green Benz and those soldiers.

"Hey, Kobi, it's Joseph."

"Hmm – you." Kobi had been labelled in many ways by those who met him. I wasn't sure about the definitions, but I did know he was my oldest friend. We'd shared our teenage years, as close as some brothers, but even by the tender age of twelve, I could see he was mostly spoiled.

"How's Sarah?"

"Who?"

"Your girlfriend, bro."

Fragments gleaned from our years together had told me why. The illegitimate child of an important Ghanaian politician, he'd been abandoned by his mother in Accra, aged two, a pawn in a frightening strategy of brinkwomanship, in which she tried to force the father to take responsibly for the boy.

"Oh Sarah. Got rid of her two months back. Women. You know." Kobi had learnt harsh lessons in survival early on being passed from relative to relative as a toddler and then at one of Ghana's best boarding schools where he was sent, aged seven, mainly to keep him at arm's length. From what he'd described, there, he had been subjected to a dazzling array of punishments devised by prefects and teachers for younger pupils, reflecting the compulsion to pay someone back for the horrors that had been inflicted on them at the same age. The whole institution ran as a game of intergenerational torture tag.

"Always more tings out there, I guess, Kobs." Familiarity started to lubricate his path towards a more even keel.

"Guess so. JJ man. I was thinking about you only the other day."

"Good thoughts, I hope."

"I only have the one kind."

And here it was, almost a different person at the end of the line but not quite. The new jovial mask had the same soulless wearer. He sounded happy to hear from me now, although I knew that if he felt things at all, it was only slightly.

Still a boy, his later school holidays had been spent in his father's Accra mansion, but here he was regularly abused by the house's maids who had nobody better to show what they'd learnt at an early age from their elders than this second-class citizen of a son.

"Just seen my mums at the hospital. She's fucked, man – doubt she'll get out." Anger at the women who bore us had always been one of the strongest unspoken bonds of our relationship. Aged eleven, he was brought to the UK to live with the distant stranger who was called his mother. He ended up in a crumbling school, sitting next to a gawky, damaged, mid-brown kid – me.

"Oh well, J – parents innit!" He hissed a sort of laugh as if a snake bite really was that funny.

"Yeah... I'm working a thing at the moment. Your kind of help would be very welcome."

At school, we hit it off instantly, the 'badness' recognised itself and we had piled up more trouble than I wanted to remember. Even back then, there was a difference between us. We both knew he would go further than I and for far less. That was why I needed him now.

Kobi paused before answering, his high-functioning brain working types of calculations I would never come close to making.

"What you after here, Joseph?"

I could have talked about racism in Britain, but he didn't care about that. He was mostly blind to it because, in Kobi's world, everyone was both hunter and hunted. He generally preferred the company of white people, as they were easier prey. They all wanted that one harmless black friend. It was a fast way in and he could be very unthreatening until you got to know him better.

"City trader needs following. Suspect he's got some bad habits."

"They mostly do. Which bank?"

Kobi fulfilled the drug-taking demands of a bunch of banker 'friends' in the City and had therefore gotten to know a lot about how it worked. He'd once told me he had his eye on trying to get a job in a hedge fund because it was by far the best scam he'd ever seen. Despite the obstacle of race and not having earned great grades at school, it wouldn't have surprised me if he made that leap one day, such were his intellectual abilities.

"GBC."

"Ah, Gresham Street then."

"His name's Wade Barker. Heads up some kind of trading desk in the investment bank. I need to see what he does after work."

"He got money?"

"There might be grease in it there but I'll probably be taking this one on account."

Four years ago, Kobi had been seeing an eighteen-year-old who turned out to be fifteen and the daughter of a policeman. Her father was less than pleased when he found out and made his opinion known to his girl with hard knuckles. After one battering, he'd told her he was coming for her 'nigger boyfriend' next. Kobi came to me for a way out of his predicament. Police were specifically difficult for a man like him because many of the attributes he possessed couldn't be fruitfully deployed against them without earning a life sentence.

I spent two weeks on the policeman day and night. I had a hunch that a man who would hit his little girl like that probably had other behavioural issues. I finally caught him only a few miles from the family home, paying a woman who'd also been someone's little girl at one time. He received the photos with a letter and that was that. Kobi even got to see the daughter whenever he wanted, but quickly tired of her as he did anyone once he'd gotten them to trust him.

"Have you got any groundwork on Señor Barker?"

"I could if you need."

"Nah it's OK. I'll get on him and call you when I get something."

"Thanks, brother. I don't know this one so can't judge how crazy he is. Some of those older white men are the most dangerous of all."

"Not of all, bro, not of all." I understood the honesty in the statement. I was sending a wolf to track a hyena.

6

MONDAY EVENING

I got to Holborn early, left a message for Kate to tell her I was working as a cleaner tonight. She knew enough to know what that meant and I gave her the name of the firm to make it sound as truthful as possible. It wasn't clear how we'd gotten to the point where I had to tell the truth about the truth. I'd not slept with other women since being with her. For Kate, it was something else, something about how I related, that made her suspicious. She'd once said I was like water: the closer you grabbed it, the less you had of it. Maybe she just had infidelity on the mind herself.

Passing the spare greenery of Lincolns Inn Fields, all around me, the legal engine room of the country hummed busily on its way to winding down for the day. Deals had been done, hours billed, criminals defended and proper money earned. Some of the suited contingent slunk off to favoured bars in Covent Garden or Aldywch before heading home. Junior associates laughed wide-eyed at the jokes of the older people they called boss, as if, somehow, seniority by itself imparted a genius of comic timing. It was a lusciously warm evening and drinking away the stresses of a well-paid London job outside was an alluring prospect.

Then later, for a few of them, there would be other diversions. I had done work for the proprietor of a brothel about a mile away, on a patron whose sexual tastes had strayed beyond the range of her already-exotic menu. I quickly found out he was untouchable, simply too well-connected, and immediately downed tools. Rita, the owner, kept an office of sorts in a bedroom onsite around the dregs of Euston. I'd advised her that she'd have to simply accept it – rotate the girls and boys to make it easier for them. Or, alternatively, bring in proper protection who might just be able to battle it out with the legal titan's associates. She knew the second option meant the equivalent of slavery for her and her stable.

I was thinking about the look on the brothel manager's face that day – resignation and disgust, at me and at the whole rotten system – when I spotted Mable going into the back entrance of Cubbins, Jacques and Heward. I'd worked quite a few of Everett's crews and knew some of the faces.

"Hey, Mabes!"

She looked up from concentrating hard on some

aspect of her experience in this life, took a second to connect my face with the job and then beamed.

"Christopher! What are you doing here, my darling?" The fifty-year-old Ghanaian refused to call me by my fake name, Chris, because she'd told me Christopher carried more weight in the world. She wanted the best for her boy.

"Am on the crew this evening innit. How's life?"

"Ah life… 'life is', as they say!"

We both smiled knowingly, went in together and Mable helped me get the necessary passes from a vaguely suspicious building manager. A few more joined us, I was introduced, we picked up the cleaning props and got to it. Nobody was giving overtime here, least of all Everett. I found Lawrence Michael's desk as Folarin had indicated, then dusted, wiped and vacuumed his floor for two hours until the last hard-working lawyer had packed up for the evening. Lawrence Michaels' bottom drawer wasn't locked. Inside sat a single A4 envelope containing a complete set of Wimbledon debenture holder tickets for each day of the two-week tennis tournament. The envelope had the words *Courtesy of R.A. Capital* scribed elegantly in red fountain pen. There was a crest underneath embossed in wax. For all the precision of the calligraphy above it, I couldn't pick out anything concrete in the melted picture.

Half an hour later, I tumbled out of the back entrance of the office with the weary crew, ghosts of concerns lingering just beyond my ability to form them into worries. If Lawrence Michaels had left thousands of pounds of centre court tickets sitting there in his drawer, his life was either in crisis or, more simply, he wasn't coming back.

Ashley was sitting on a low metal fence a hundred metres away looking suspicious, ignoring instructions intended to avoid this happening. We could have been mistaken for brothers, sharing a lean stature and shades of skin about the same caramel brown, but we had been forged in different kilns. There was more than a hint of fear in the dizzy way his head twisted itself towards me. He stood with some effort, movements a touch rubbery, suggesting less strength in the frame than there should be.

"Hey, Jo, long time!"

I put away my annoyance for now.

"Ashley! How's tings"?

He glanced down as a gust of shame wafted into view.

"Hard, bruv, hard. Seems like I've been on these streets a while now."

"You still with Cushnie?"

"Not really – nah. We parted ways. By mutual consent, as they say." He flinched at the memory of the exit interview with the underworld gatekeeper.

Ashley didn't look high or in withdrawal this evening. His clothes were clean enough to pass but his jacket was ripped at the sleeve – there probably wasn't another. I imagined he had lots of time on his hands.

"I need you to watch a flat for me in Hackney for a few days. It's off Kingsland Road, about a mile past Shoreditch. Thirty pounds a day. Be there before 8:30am, leave at 7:30pm. I can bring you in on more of my things if you do this one properly. There's good money in it sometimes."

Unexpected bonuses occasionally revealed themselves, which was a major reason to stay in touch with people like Cushnie. You never knew when you might need to buy or sell something along the way. Everett had made a down payment of three hundred thousand pounds for saving his business and he knew that was cheap at the price.

My old school friend laboured at the brink of the new reality for our relationship. He was a bit older, but things were what they were and money for doing the nothing that he'd be doing anyway sounded good. He needed to make the mental trip quickly because my balcony nightcap wouldn't wait long.

"I've gotta go. Call me, Ashley. Tomorrow when you get there. I'll send the details."

His eyes betrayed a mixture of confusion, resentment and fear of losing out.

"Now's not the time, bro. I'm properly knackered! We can catch up later." I handed him a sixty-pound advance because I wanted to see what he'd spent it on by tomorrow.

7

TUESDAY

The deep green of Southwest London, housing the world's oldest tennis tournament, was less than ten miles from Peckham Rye. It was my first time through one of the high gates into a dazzling circus of events put on for those with hundreds of pounds to spend on a day out. For some with thousands to burn, though, there was an even better experience to be had in the debenture holders' lounges. I had put on cream cotton trousers, white cross trainers and, under a dark-blue windbreaker, a white silk mix I'd picked up from a Bangladeshi shirt seller in Whitechapel. Around my neck hung one of Lawrence Michaels' debenture badges, which got me into the even more privileged bit of the show without any questions. Climbing many flights of square-winding stairs delivered me to a small rooftop bar where glasses of alcohol went for the prices of bottles.

My gaze stretched out over sun-blessed minor courts where less successful players were plying their trade, chased frantically by the twin demons of what might happen for them one day and the rising possibility of what might not.

Excited conversations buzzed around me, fuelled by the gladiatorial contests to come, fine sun and expensive alcohol. A note in the envelope I'd stolen from Lawrence Michaels' desk suggested this was where the R.A. Capital party would find themselves between matches. The young serving staff were unusual. They were all Caucasian, equipped with accents that would soon place them on the other side of the transactions they were making. This wasn't a gig for which Everett might supply bodies anytime soon. Here, the sons and daughters of the tennis establishment were simply staking a claim on their valuable futures at an appropriately early moment.

The day's centre court match programme commenced, and I watched it from a wall-hung television, resisting the temptation to find the seat that neither I nor Lawrence Michaels would be occupying. As the floor thinned out, a well-heeled teenager smiled his way up to me from behind the bar emboldened by home advantage.

"You prefer to miss the first set? Yeah, I know I do too, man, but don't tell my mum that – she'd never speak to me again!"

I smiled as conspiratorially as I could at the kid.

"I was just taking in the atmosphere."

"First time here?"

"No, but first time up here," I lied once only.

"Who's your favourite then?"

"Easy. Serena Williams. She has everything as far as I can see."

A trace of disapproval tinged his frown as my words registered but then he smiled in conspiracy once again.

"I'm a Federer man myself."

"Well, you know Roger himself says Serena is the greatest ever."

The boy shrugged uncomfortably knowing he was right but worried that explaining exactly why could end badly. I needed to put him at ease.

"But they are all great and we are blessed to have them. Listen, could you get me an iced coffee?"

He relaxed back on safe territory and strode off with great purpose to perform the job he knew he'd not be doing in two years' time. I wouldn't be able to stay here all match now, which complicated things only slightly given the number of venues available in this privileged part of The Lawn Tennis Association's money-making dream. I floated through restaurants and balconies where the rich home counties came every year to celebrate the wealth that they accumulated through inheritance, hard work or just plain luck.

When the first match was done, I climbed the stairs once again to the top bar, behind a shaven-headed young black man wearing an exquisitely tailored sky-blue jacket. Within in a minute, I knew he was the reason I'd come.

"Hey, guys, what you having? Shall we just get a bottle of something white and see where it goes?" he shouted towards two older white men seated at a table a metre from where I had earlier stood.

"Sounds good, Flo!"

'Flo' – a shortening of Nigerian names I'd heard before, this version a less threatening task for English-speaking tongues. He stood about six foot tall, gym-trained, and had that easy confidence possessed by those who'd attended the same schools as the white men who sat waiting for the drink he'd purchased. I nodded to my new friend, the bar boy, took my glass of expensive sparkling water to watch the failing players on the minor courts and listened.

The three were soon joined by two more men in their forties, the cuts of their jackets doing the harder work of hiding fat rather than accentuating the muscle underneath. Flo was as at home here as a shark in the ocean.

"Henri Chevalier – good to see you! How the devil are the clients at Banque de Montagne?" He said the name with a flawless French accent to the older well-attired money man.

"They're good. They've had some excellent advice, it seems." Henri smiled enigmatically in self-congratulation at some inside joke.

The group toasted the day as if they'd created it and the discussion wound around the shit men talked about when together and about which I rarely saw the point.

Three of the five were guests: people with something to offer, the fifth seemed to be Lawrence Michaels' last-minute replacement. From various listening points, I admired the Nigerian in action. His performance was charisma laced with humility, likeable and knowledgeable in equal parts – a perfection of salesmanship.

They ordered two follow-ups, waiting for the second set to develop before heading courtside. The day's sunshine intensified, elevating the fine surroundings as I drifted again from court to court witnessing the parallel economic universe on broad display only thirty minutes' drive from my own.

Back upstairs after match number two, the R.A. Capital group became rowdier under the encouragement of a further bottle.

"You know, at school, this fellow here, Flo Danjuma, was even captain of the rugby team, but he had only one weakness – you know what it was?" The three guests leaned in to hear which heel the modern-day Achilles could be cut from.

"He just couldn't ever take his drink! Do you remember, Flo… maybe a little bit perhaps…?"

Flo Danjuma. The other R.A. Capital employee had known the Nigerian at school.

"No, no! Taylor, please don't!" Playing to the audience, doing his part to build up to the punch line.

"…Falling into the pond half-clothed outside the house master's cottage?"

Flo was uncovered; they all laughed hilariously and, meanwhile, the listener in their midst felt the rising cold. It was a feeling I knew well. The poisonous gas of lack that many who grew up where I had secretly cherished. We'd breathed it in early on and held it closely to our chests, like a child's comforter; so close it had merged with us inside and become a part of the reason we couldn't ever go beyond the invisible walls set by a country that claimed to have none. The lethal substance metamorphosed into a shooting envy. It demanded in anguish over and over *why him, not me?* I didn't need these silly boys' tales from a boarding school I would never see!

"You know, Viner hinted something's gotten stuck in your West African operations. Nigeria?"

Viner. The name had been uttered with a trace of fear and it brought me back to my senses, tuning me in immediately like an eagle spotting its hare from a mile away. The conversation diminished to almost a whisper.

"Nigeria's OK actually – insurgents still leaving us well alone for a price. It's Ghana where there's an issue. We may need help with your contacts in the foreign office. I don't know for sure yet, but Viner feels it's worth a heads up just in case."

"Trouble with the locals?" The third guest joined the fray. I got the feeling he would have used the term 'natives' had Flo not been there. The young Nigerian probably had the same thought but carried on as if oblivious to it.

"It can get pretty complex out there at times. But we have some friendly lawmakers on side thanks to you, judge."

Flo's colleague, Taylor, cleared his throat, suggesting things had gone as far as they should in these surroundings.

"Taylor's right. Let's talk about this on Friday's call, gentlemen. We may have a clearer view by then."

The men leaned back in a fog of alcohol-blemished thought for a minute before plans for the evening's supper resurrected their capacity for speech.

I left quietly to get well ahead in the taxi queue outside. On the way out of the debenture holders' area, wealthy retirees, dressed in their Wimbledon finery, staggered about on unsteady legs, having given up the battle for sobriety with the day's alcoholic offerings.

My taxi chugged into action destined for the Mayfair restaurant where the group were heading next. I had information now. Enough to formulate questions and make connections. I called Frank Okello, the Ugandan computer genius who was what you might call my secret weapon.

Frank had come out of university with a first-class degree and quickly gotten into trouble with the authorities, which saw him being sectioned under the Mental Health Act. His sister rang me for help and we went to visit him at one of the two types of British institutions where the most talented young men of his race often ended up. Frank was discharged into the care of his sister after I found some dirt on the psychiatrist in charge of his case, which swayed his clinical opinion a bit. I promised him that Frank would take the medication, which to my knowledge he still did. I didn't charge Frank's sister because her brother was as valuable to me as a prophylactic in a Zimbabwean brothel.

"Hey, Okello!"

"Mr Wright." It was a feature of his condition to be formal.

"How's it?"

"Fine." Frank wasn't big on small talk, which was one of many things I found liberating about dealing with him. Whatever brain differences he possessed also conferred world-class software abilities and an obsessive focus on assigned tasks.

"I need you to check out a few connected names for me. Everything you can get as soon as you can, please." As a consequence of liking formality, Frank responded very well to good manners.

"Yes, of course."

"And, Frank, please tread carefully. We really don't want these to know we are here."

"Understood, Mr Wright."

I disconnected, sat back in the worn seating of the of the unroadworthy black cab and texted him names.

RA Capital and a boss called Viner, Cubbins Jacques & Heward and a lawyer working for the firm named Lawrence Michaels who is off work, Banque de

Montagne, Flo Danjuma, Henri Chevalier, Yaw Asante, who has disappeared in Cubbins' employ. Tunde Folarin, our new client who is looking for Asante and works there too. Someone called Taylor who might work for any of the three organisations.

Some part of me clenched as it always did seeing the caller's name jangle into view on my phone like a Halloween advert.

"I've got something."

"Kobi."

"I am outside Lucy's in Hackney. Our man Wade Barker likes his strippers. He had supper in a curry house with some mid-level banker types then they headed here. I would go in but I don't want to get spotted."

"Spotted? What, you and strippers?"

"I had a slight misunderstanding a couple of years back with a gentleman who now works security here. He got injured. Not sure if he's working inside tonight."

Slight misunderstanding. I easily imagined what might have happened but it couldn't have been so bad because the bouncer was still able to find employment after his wounds had healed.

"Bet our man's married and likes more than strippers. Speak tomorrow before midday." Kobi didn't need any directing. He sounded like he was actually having fun as far as anyone like him could.

I spent the rest of the evening feeling the caress of a June breeze on my cheeks, reclining in one of Mayfair's garden squares. From here I watched the Nigerian and two remaining guests taste good food, excrete loud laughs and sip expertly selected wines. Only a few homeless people seemed to want to make this square their bedroom tonight and those that did instinctively knew enough to stay away from me. The meal done, Danjuma bade his guests a warm goodnight and walked briskly south west, past the backside of Buckingham Palace to the lovely Knightsbridge mews he called home. I stood for a while in the shadows watching his front door, aware that I needed to go to sleep but drawn to the flame of a life which somehow seemed so utterly impossible for someone like me. I knew the answer to the question, of course. It was simply fate. He was born to this and I wasn't.

8

WEDNESDAY

"Hi, Kate."

"Joseph. Jesus, it's 5am!"

"Sorry – just checking in. You free any nights coming up?"

"Yeah, yeah. I'll send you a message once I've actually woken up."

"A really dirty one, I hope. Have a good day 'girlfriend'." The sarcasm of my last word was lost on her in the shock waves of the morning's premature launch towards the summit of South London's estate agency sector.

I made another call. She wasn't asleep yet.

"Del, it's Joseph." Delores Machado was deciding if she should hang up for a whole number of reasons going back to our late teens.

"Can I come round to see you? Still across from the police station?"

She exhaled a sigh with real depth like you do when you step in something a dog has left on the pavement.

"What do you want, Joseph?"

There was no point in lying.

"I'm after a man who likes the girls at Lucy's. Do you know where he might go afterwards and who with?" Soon after we broke up, my former girlfriend had fallen on even harder times than I did. She ended up selling looks at her young body out of clubs dotted around the outskirts of the City of London.

I had gotten her out of a scrape a year before with a regular who very much wanted to become her friend. Delores had watched a recording of me using a hammer on some of his fingers, learning far more about me that evening than she had during our few years together. There was something about the balding English stalker. The savagery he'd probably experienced as a child had produced a rawness in him that both scared and infuriated me. I had perhaps gone too far but how far is that when you have a killer who doesn't know it yet sitting opposite you? She'd never wanted to be anywhere near me after that.

I didn't care because once the memory of extreme pain had subsided, I was sure the stalker's evil spirits would return to dominate their host. And so just in case, I left him an aide-memoire. The book contained pictures of Delores's stalker trying to lick the pants off a friend of my ex-girl. It contained images of his stockbroker boss, the flat that he couldn't afford, given the amount he was spending on Delores, and finally, his ageing mother picking out fruit at the supermarket. A man with the drives I perceived in him wouldn't be able to stop, would very likely get worse without treatment. He had to be so scared of me that he would move on from Delores to the next girl. I still had Frank Okello keep tabs on the emerging maniac every few months.

"What's his name?" She knew she owed me.

"Wade Barker – works for Global Banking Corporation."

"Poor guy." I said nothing. We both knew this was true.

"I'll ask around and call you. Then I don't want to hear from you anymore."

I couldn't promise that so waited until she'd disconnected.

The overnight rain had helped the morning impart a crispness to objects that had been lacking in preceding days. I was sitting fifty metres from Danjuma's mews before he left for work. His day job took him back around where he'd eaten supper and into a discreet stone-clad entrance a few metres up from the visual fantasies of luxury offered in New Bond Street's shop windows.

You had to ring to be let in through heavy glass doors. A brass roster on the wall behind the reception bore vague descriptions of the type of services that the wealthy foreigner might need in London once they'd dropped thousands on some glamorous items in the boutiques nearby:

Wealth Management.
Property Management.
Investment Administration.

The young woman whose job it was to sit and do very little all day reminded me of Kate. She played her role well, smiling professionally as I approached. Mayfair wasn't prejudiced in the usual way, not upfront at least. Almost anyone could join the club as long as they bought in and you never knew how much money a young black man in a blue hoodie might command until you were looking after that money for him.

"Excuse me, I am looking for R.A. Capital – can't see 'em up there."

The receptionist was confused. "No, sorry, we don't have that one here, sir." She looked a nice woman and a twang to her accent told me she probably still lived somewhere that I would find familiar. I took a small risk.

"Sorry, but I saw that bald-headed black guy coming in before me – thought I knew him from R.A. when I was there… his name's Joseph Akande."

"No, that's Mr Danjuma, he works on the fifth floor at Banque de Montagne."

"Argh, really sorry for the mistake! Sorry for the time-wasting too."

She returned my smile without question and I was reminded why I'd fallen for Kate a year ago. The promise of straightforwardness, someone saying what they meant and turning up when they said, must have seemed very attractive back then.

My client answered his phone cautiously. "Yes? Mr Wright?"

"Did Yaw Asante have any money issues or was it just a way back to Accra?"

He didn't hesitate.

"The second. He'd lost everything there, so it would cost to rebuild." Folarin was quickly growing on me. His intellect allowed him to bypass the usual patterns of ego and get straight to the point.

"His wife had recently died."

"Yes. They weren't close anymore. How can you be after so many years apart? But it… it made him feel like he didn't want to die in Britain. Not here, a place where he'd only come to hide."

"Would he have needed some high-up friends to return?"

"Hard to say – depends on why he really left. He was investigating a few powerful men, but maybe he had been taking money too. In those days in Ghana, it was very chaotic. Like Nigeria now. Everyone was stealing something."

"Everyone who mattered." I let the afterthought

dangle in the mix with an image of the Knightsbridge pied-à-terre, which Flo Danjuma called home. "So, there might be an outstanding legal case against Yaw Asante somewhere. You'd need a lawyer or two onside for that one."

"It was a long time ago, but the worst people have good memories." Folarin now sounded like he was talking more about his own sorrowful position than his friend's.

"I will get back to you when there's something more to say."

I flexed the anxiety out of my neck. R.A. Capital may not have been Danjuma's day job but it was still his bread and butter.

The voicemail was on.

Hi, Everett. Is there any way I could access Banque de Montagne's Mayfair branch office one evening soon?

My final call of the morning went to Ashley Adebayo, probably wondering if he'd get paid for sitting around outside Yaw Asante's place in Hackney.

"Hey, how's it going over there?"

"Nothing, bruv. Not even any dealers. Things are proper shit here."

"It's the end of the line. When you're done, meet me at mine about 9pm. I'll send a text when I'm on the way. And keep things low-key."

Danjuma strode purposefully out some time around 11:30, and I followed him to a tailor where he was having a jacket fitted by ageing English men who could have been working there for two hundred years. Then on to a late lunch at an outside table with a beautiful, soon-to-be-old woman. The head waiter smiled respectfully when Danjuma spoke and serving staff moved around them swiftly, efficiently attending to wants and needs. Flo's lunch date treated him like he was a nephew, but she faintly wished for more without bitterness, such were his gifts in relating to others.

A voice erupted too close to my left ear.

"Any chance of a thousand quid, mate?"

I frowned at the brazen beggar, wondering how he'd managed to get the jump on me as the dry aldehyde of envy was working its way into every organ.

"Why not? It is Mayfair, you know!"

We both smiled at the craziness of it all.

For the rest of the afternoon, Grosvenor Square saw speculations entwine with languid sunbeams in an uncomfortable dance of uncertainty. Who was R.A. Capital and what might some old European bank and a British law firm have to do with them? How had a lowly security guard ended up being kidnapped by mercenaries? Finally, what was the problem in Ghana and was that related to Asante's disappearance? The mobile ringer sounded only once.

"Jolene!" Kobi's nickname for me at school came from a Dolly Parton country song. I never knew why and perhaps that was the whole point, but it told me he was in a playful mood.

"Hi, K. How's our stripper-lover doing?"

"I have his address, photos of his wife and the two twenty-something kids. He lives in Wanstead near Epping Forest. It's nice out there." I understood the threat to Barker's family that the second piece of information implied but chose to ignore it for now.

"Happy families. Guess I'll go have a chinwag with him. Can you email me the pictures?"

"You want me there for that chat?" The way my friend said *chat* invited a battalion of worries.

"Umm – he show any sign of violence?"

"He's crazy enough to spend his hard-earned dough in Lucy's. You never know with people, do you?" I weighed up the fear Kobi could instil in anyone with the damage he might do to Wade Barker if they came face to face.

"I'll have a think but don't wanna waste you on unnecessary stuff."

"OK, Jolene – in your court. Just one more thing." There was always a price to pay somewhere with Kobi, even if you didn't know what it was at the time.

"Do you think your mums knew she was going crazy before she did? I mean, did she ever talk about it?"

"Yeah, I think so, and she was scared too. She suffered, bro. Mostly I remember she suffered."

Kobi clicked off, seeming to have obtained what he wanted. At 6pm, the man I was following made a short walk to the designer gym he used to keep in shape for those lady clients, a place where the monthly bill would swallow the average Londoner's disposable income. I left him in there honing well-manicured muscle and took a long bus through the sun-blessed city towards my balcony.

The childlike drug user, who had now adjusted to considering himself my employee, was hanging about at the entrance to the flats. He shifted around, navigating the tiny semicircle of pain that was his addiction, and I decided not to hand over any cash just yet.

"Ashley – come up for a drink, bro." He looked like he had somewhere else to be and I decided to test how badly.

"Nah, listen, man, I gotta get…"

"Where've you gotta be, Ash? Really?" The look I gave him let him know this wasn't negotiable. "Just have a brandy with me like old friends do, then you can go on your way."

We stood silently arm to arm, trying to ignore the atmosphere of piss and disinfectant that meant the council considered it had done its job cleaning the lift. He knew the way from there and I pulled a chair from my small living room out to the balcony. The summer evening's calm had melted over the Rye, making it feel like a seaside holiday.

"Your dad's an arsehole, I get that."

The boyish man nearly toppled off the chair I'd

offered him. He shot me a questioning look but knew it wouldn't be enough.

"He's more than that, Joseph. He's a fucking psycho. You know what he used to do to my mums before I left… you know?"

"I can imagine, my friend. I've seen that video."

"Maybe you do know, maybe you don't, but I was in there with it from young, bro – watching it from time!"

I nodded without emotion and took a sip of the fine alcohol that I owned.

"The thing is that from where I stand, I see plenty of us that just had proper nonsense for parents, Ashley, and we all know it too. It's not like we are sitting here saying 'my mums was the best, she was always there for me… blah blah blah'. We know they are bags of shite. So, my question to you, Ashley Adebayo, is: given we know it, why can't we seem to be able to recover from them? You've got whatever you've got that's making you jumpy right now. What is it, spice?"

He didn't answer because there wasn't one, had never been any that made sense. A bitter grin creased my mouth conjured by an image of the fine wines Flo Danjuma had libated twenty-four hours earlier.

"And I've got my trustee warm French mistress here." I carefully gathered up the bottle of cognac and poured him another.

Ashley glanced up, pleading eyes, frozen by terrible memories. He needed to escape this: escape me, before I got too drunk, but he knew I could keep him there as long as I pleased. His right leg started jerking uncontrollably in the chair, shoulders squirming. I carried on, pretending to be oblivious to my guest's worsening condition. My new employee was to me what I was to Danjuma, and I wanted him to feel it: the shame I had experienced at Flo's privileged hand.

"Well, come on! What do you think about it, bruv? What's your answer?" I growled the last words as if failure to reply meant real danger. The child-man fixed me squarely with hollow eyes.

"I… I try not to think about it at all, Joseph. I just don't want to go back there ever – you know?"

Ashley's powerlessness had me feeling high and happy now. The cognac was good enough to write any story.

"Yeah, Ashley. Yeah. Right there, you've got it, boy. That, my friend, is the answer! We try so hard to forget what they did that we end up forgetting everything, including who we are and what we are here to do!" I sighed and chuckled in parallel as if hearing a touching anecdote from the past. Ashley stared glumly into space.

"Alright, alright. You gotta go. I know. Thanks for the chat. Be there every day around 8am for the next week. I don't wanna have to come and check up on you."

I handed him ten twenty-pound notes. His kidnapping at an end, the addict's eyes blazed intensely at the three-figure sum.

"Cool, bro, cool. I… I won't let ya down."

I looked gravely at the loose body containing my old school friend.

"Don't!"

He slammed the door shut on the way out as if he never wanted it open again and my body relaxed backwards, taking in the artistry of the wine maker's artificial high.

"**H**ey, Kate, wassup?"

There was no hesitation this time – she sounded unusually happy to hear from me.

"Joseph! Where are you?"

"Oh, just on the balcony thinking about my gal! How about you come over tonight? It's not so late?"

"How about Friday evening, hun?"

"Hard day at work?"

"Let's just say they get their money's worth out of us."

"That's capitalism for you."

"You know it, darlin'!"

I cut off and felt the dance of loneliness tugging at my guts. Scattering my attention away from it towards another few tumblers of cognac quickly brought the warm mystery of sleep.

was awakened by a muffled cry somewhere in the flat and came into the green-painted hallway, whose walls throbbed into me as I made the short trip to the living room. It seemed to take an age to navigate. There was a mellow orange light on in the room as I entered. The kitchen to the right looked tidy as I had left it. Then I saw the hulking frame of my father seated in a vest, khaki shorts and sandals. He looked up at me with vacant eyes and the taste of faeces wafted from underneath. He had messed himself on our couch. I nodded towards the open door of the balcony and he knew what this meant. It was time. There was a whoosh of air as a large brown body fell into the night. I looked down at the receding shit-stained shorts of a man who fell gratefully towards the concrete.

9

THURSDAY MORNING

"So you see, you don't need to hit him so hard. Just in the right place with enough body weight in it but not too much. Just the amount that gives you the balance to come away from him or go again if you need to."

The ponytailed Persian fight trainer came out of a punching demonstration to underline the point. There were three or four newer lads, but the rest had been here for at least five years. We called ourselves 'the old-timers', none over thirty and still we knew very little about each other beyond those basics. Poorang had grown a small pot belly into middle age but it would have been dangerous to be fooled by it.

"If you put it all into the one blow, it's like betting it all on one horse. Worse because you don't know exactly what will happen even if your ticket crosses the line first. He might have a very hard jaw. Argh, what is it with the horse analogy!"

We all laughed shyly. Poorang was our teacher, our leader, and we knew, if all else failed us, he would be our carer too. There'd been more than one of his boys put up on the sofa and quite a few hospitals visited over the years when his first mantra, 'don't get caught', had been misapplied.

"And if you have to get involved like this, what's rule number two?"

We shouted in cult-like unison.

"Breathe, always; you can't do shit if you don't."

After the lesson, I headed towards him and waited until others had paid their respects.

"Joseph." He always looked at me with something akin to a knowing wariness. Maybe he regretted taking on that thirteen-year-old, but if they existed, those feelings never escaped beyond that first glance.

"Hey, Poorang. I was wondering. You came from Iran, right, in 1979?"

He hesitated to consider why the question had been asked. I wasn't sure he liked me.

"My parents did, you mean. I was much younger than you when you first came to see me."

"Do you ever want to go back there? Britain's hard, man. I mean, for immigrants."

"I see where you're coming from now. I don't myself because it's not the country I would want it to be. That doesn't mean I don't miss the feeling of…"

"Belonging?"

"Yeah that's it. I see my family here and, in the US, thinking about Iran with rose-tinted glasses. That's always dangerous. You go back like that, and you'll be eaten alive by whatever system you wished you knew but don't."

"There's powerful people here too running their game on everyone just like in Iran."

"That's true but here I mostly have a choice over whether to keep my distance from them. Over there, I'm not so sure. In Iran, someone powerful wants you for something, you're done one way or another."

"Sounds like working for Cushnie."

"Yes, but even that has a choice in it somewhere at the start, even if the youngsters don't fully understand it at the time." I nodded my thanks for his wisdom, which he reciprocated with eyes that had softened some.

"I always wondered how you avoided that route, Joseph – the Cushnie path. You got the brain and the… you know, the 'other abilities' to be very valuable to somebody like him."

"I'm a loner, Poorang. People like Cushnie need herd animals. They are more controllable."

I was outside Delores's door before the morning made eleven. She was a resident of a ten-floor block similar to my own, except it overlooked the local police headquarters. This added an unbalancing mixture of both comfort and menace, the proportions depending on who you were. I hesitated before dialling.

"Hi, D, I'm outside." She opened almost instantly and surveyed me with a combination of hostility and pain. The bright living room shared similar dimensions to my own but was tastefully decorated in yellow and pine. She'd placed a large vase of sunflowers on the kitchen worktop.

"Do you want a tea or coffee?" The offer would have been real if she could've urinated in it.

"No, thanks."

When she turned around to get her mug, I looked my former girlfriend up and down. The job was keeping her fit and those South American genes had made a beautiful woman from the teenager I'd left nine years earlier. The weight of a disappointing life was another matter. Her eyes told that story.

"So does anyone know Wade Barker?" I used precise words to deflect from the reality of what I was asking. If the life she'd fallen into meant she knew women who sold their bodies, whose fault might that have been?

"Yeah they do."

"What's he saying?"

"He's rough and mean, not tender at all."

"A regular?" Her neck sat back slightly, witnessing once again the lack of emotion with which I pursued my chosen profession.

"Once a week maybe. He doesn't ever tip, so he likely doesn't have that much money."

"He have any favourite stuff… or any dodgy requests?"

"None mentioned beyond the bully shit – but that's not unusual."

"Any friends that are also regulars?"

"He hangs with a bunch of banker types – you know – fat, middle-aged, bald. They like to get drunk and then be the men they fantasise about, but never were. Poor arseholes."

"All white?"

"Don't know, but from the sounds of him, that would likely be the case."

"So does he have a favourite girl for after?"

"I didn't ask."

I kept quiet, needing her to get there without me.

"You want me to ask? Fuck, Joseph, I told you this was it!"

"I heard you, but I promise this is for a good cause." She was getting angrier and those ripples would soon become squalls needing to crash themselves out. I took some of Delores's flower-touched air in, then let it out slower.

"A good cause, a good cause! What about my cause, Joseph? Where the fuck were you for that one? After the abortion clinic, eh? Or when my puta of a ma booted me out? Where were you?" In that moment, she looked like she was reliving a condensed version of all the frustration and loneliness. There was nothing I could say that would help. I stared blankly, breathing deliberately. Finally, it came down to that one question.

"Where were you, Joseph?"

Her pain caused a folding in me and I stared straight up into it.

"I understand that it was difficult for you, Delores. I can imagine this because it was for me at that time too. I had a mother on the way back to the mental ward, no money, no hope for the future. What choices did I have really? I had to become like this – had to make the decisions I did, to survive. And I understand, in fact, I know, so did you. We made it through and here we are."

The pot of hurt that had Delores pacing wall to wall reduced a touch with the unveiling of simple truths. I kept focused on her for a few minutes more, so she'd know I'd meant what I had said.

"Delores, after this, we will be done."

She nodded and kept herself looking down in homage maybe to the thing that had just happened, or to things ten years ago. I couldn't tell but I knew enough to get up and leave the sunny room to the person who'd succeeded in making it that way.

10

THURSDAY AFTERNOON

"Hey, Uncle." For some reason, the title of 'Uncle' still felt right.

"Joseph."

Clients usually asked questions, but something towards the core of Uncle Ernest didn't want to, so I answered anyway.

"I am planning a small chat with our man Wade Barker tonight but thought I would give you a last chance to pull out."

A room of silence needed filling.

"I will do my best to contain things, but once I start, you never know where they could end up. I owe it to you to make you understand this. Should I go ahead?"

During his silence, frustration nudged its way impatiently into the area where compassion had briefly sat.

"Uncle Ernest. Should I?"

"You know, Jojo, when we came to this country…"

"In the early '80s."

"Yes, thirty years ago. We had plans of becoming in some ways like them. The British, I mean. Not exactly. We are ourselves. But we thought just living a certain way would be enough; that we would be offered some opportunities… the ones they had…. in the end."

"Your generation and the one before it were heroes, Uncle. The ones that stayed, I mean, not the others who scarpered back home."

He made a grunt with his throat at the not-so-subtle reference to my father.

"Back in 1983, the government was telling everyone to buy their house. So, I went to my local bank branch on Peckham High Street to see about getting a mortgage. We had a double income, and we didn't want to buy our council flat. We were aiming further than that – wanted to get away from the whole environment."

I'd not witnessed the man at the end of the line ever get irritable, let alone annoyed.

"You know what happened, Jojo?"

I could guess but let him carry on.

"The bank manager looked at me sitting there that day. I will never forget the smirk on his face as he told me I would only be eligible for the local authority housing loan scheme. I was too 'risky' for the 'mainstream market'. *Too risky for the mainstream market.* He used the term but we both understood what he meant. You know the name of that bank, Jojo?"

"Now let me see. Global Banking Corporation?"

"Please go ahead with Wade Barker, son."

As he put the phone down, I was aware of a giddiness, from being called someone's 'son'. But I was nobody's child, not in the real meaning of the word. Uncle Ernest had simply used the word because he was asking me to do something hard for him. I was a commodity to be risked in the service of more valuable people – the ones he really loved.

I ducked my head and stepped into the train that would take me north from Peckham Rye, prowling through gently drumming carriages, trying to catch the eye of anyone who might be in the mood for trouble. There were no takers, so I eventually sat down opposite a shaven-headed youth holding the lead of a fierce-looking dog, glancing up at him until he moved elsewhere.

Temper slowly dissolved in the train's nurturing motion, which allowed focus to return to things as they stood. After a while, I messaged Wade Barker two photos. The first had him entering, the second leaving, Lucy's Strip Club. The reel held plenty more, but there was no point exposing a hand that didn't need to be shown.

I left the train at Dalston Junction station, jogging past dusty windows of the haircare and food sellers who still catered primarily to an African customer despite the area's growing focus on more monied wallets. It was early, so I took the longer route up the ungentrified end of the Balls Pond Road towards Newington Green. Turning right onto Mildmay Park, my speed quickened as the many versions of poverty written in building form magically transformed into prosperity through the stroke of the property developer's pen. Air, atrophied by humid pollution, slowed me down only a little until the destination came into view.

Newington Green managed to suggest that it formed a focal part of some wealthy tree-lined village in the sticks, when in reality it was merely a patch of grass at the centre of a busy inner city roundabout. But the mini park offered a certain comfort. From inside, there was a full 365-degree line of sight and fifteen seconds to get running if the day suddenly went bad. I perched onto the back of a wooden bench and found Kobi's number. He sounded calmer today, almost wistful, a mood for which someone might have to pay later in the evening.

"Hey, Joseph."

"Kobs."

"You ever think we should just go back to the motherland to try things out there?"

"It ain't my motherland, bro. My mother's white. Plus your mother … she chose to live here for as long as you've been alive. Strictly speaking, there's no motherland in West Africa for either of us."

Not many people could get away with talking to

him like this without reprisal, but I was one of those few. I knew his story, had lived it with him and had seen many times how he liked to romanticise Ghana, the source of his childhood agony. After a dangerous pause, Kobi returned to his line of thought.

"It's just English people, the ones I know here, my friends."

"Your friends?"

"OK. Acquaintances. They want me to be a certain way, to act the drug dealer or the pimp, the cartoon character we are all fed. They aren't ever gonna let me be who I am and if I ever am that way, they get fucking scared. Ghana wasn't like that."

"You were eleven when you left, Kobi. Are you sure?"

"Yes. In Ghana, I can be the craziest motherfucker out there, but when the police catch me and beat me, they'll be beating one of their own – you know, a real person, not some creation of a coon in their heads."

I flinched at the logic of wanting to be beaten for the right reason, while instinctively surveying the fake loveliness of Newington Green. A group of mothers had arrived, prammed-up and chatting while their toddlers engaged the wonder of the climbing frame.

"I've been feeling lately, my brother, that we keep looking in the wrong places to explain why we ended up how we are – why we became what we did. Maybe we are trying to avoid the harm of the thing. The truth."

"Harm?"

"I don't know, K, it's just that I've come to believe that I would probably mostly feel the way I do anywhere: Peckham, Nigeria, the fucking Garden of Eden. It won't change. White people, black people or any people."

Kobi went as quiet as an old cemetery.

"You may be right. That's why I keep you around, Joseph. You tell me the shit I forget that I know."

There was a break in which I could hear the faint sound of his breathing. I knew well enough to let it alone in these moments.

"What's happened with the banker?"

"Hoping to hook up with our head trader this evening sometime. Maybe we can persuade him to give us a loan." Any concern for Wade Barker's well-being had drifted away with Uncle Ernest's denied mortgage. Barker surely would have some money stashed and what did I care if Kobi messed him up a bit?

"Where?"

"If it does happen, it will be in that park round the back of Brick Lane. Will confirm the details before four."

As if on cue, a text arrived from Wade Barker.

"Ah, here he is! See you later, K."

Who is this and what do you want?

The tone of the message was indignant. Not the type of emotion I'd hoped for but I pushed on anyway.

Meet me at 7pm by the entrance to Spitalfields City Farm.

OK.

Those two single letters sent spikes of worry washing into my body. These were involuntary signallers of threat, fashioned during an infancy most people wouldn't want to remember, but upon which I had long come to rely. Your average banker didn't usually agree to meet a blackmailer at a deserted park without a panicky plea or second question. The guy likely had a plan for me, which meant he had brought in other people or, worse, had total faith in the potency of his own capacity for violence.

I suggest you come alone. We will know if you don't.

Sure. See you then.

And almost casual this time, like he was looking forward to it. I sat predator still, racing through possibilities, each with its own set of contingencies, until the jerky jangly walk of Frank Okello approached from the northbound artery of Green Lanes.

Change of plan, Kobi. Will confirm later but 6pm at the park is off. Meet 6:30pm Liverpool Street, Bishopsgate side.

The man who was my only real colleague wore tight black American jeans, totally unsuited to the stifling summer day. On top there was an over-washed black T-shirt, sporting some faded Japanese manga character.

"Frank."

The Ugandan looked more nervous than usual although his afflictions made him a hard read.

"Mr Wright. I will get straight to it." Okello handed over a small blue notebook from his back pocket.

"You've been busy."

He sat totally parallel to me on the bench, turning his neck ninety degrees from time to time but mostly spoke forward as if to the invisible spirit of Newington Green. I flicked through the small book, which contained a series of precisely drafted network-based drawings, arrows connecting the names which sat at each node.

"Have you heard of The Royal African Company?"

"Pieces. I like reading history. It gives me the feeling that things that happen aren't so important really. Hadn't connected it to this though."

"The company was set up in 1660 by the king's family, the Stuarts. This was after Charles II was reinstated, his father Charles I having been beheaded in 1649. The Stuarts were partnered by the real men of power in Britain at the time, the merchants of the City of London. It was granted a monopoly of slave trading on the West African coast for a while, but successor companies diversified its portfolio of activities to gold and silver."

Okello crocked his head my way to give emphasis.

"You understand, Mr Wright? The company was owned by the richest, most powerful people in Britain and was for a time the biggest slave transporter across the Atlantic."

I nodded gloomily, noticing a caustic quality that the elixir of knowledge had produced from only one sip.

"Once its monopoly license was revoked and after several bankruptcies, most accounts suggest it was dying out by 1750 and disappeared when slavery was made illegal but…"

"Maybe it didn't?"

"Its owners in the City of London have lasted a thousand years. So, on a hunch, I gained access to some company registries. A Caribbean domiciled entity, Royal Africa Holdings, the ultimate owner of our R.A. Capital, seems to have made a number of purchases in both Ghana and Nigeria many decades ago."

"When?"

"In Ghana, it was the first half of 1964. In Nigeria, a few months later."

"What did it buy?"

Okello twisted his neck again, chiselled features impassive and robotic under thick rectangular spectacle frames.

"Land, lots of land. Thousands of hectares. In Nigeria, it was mainly towards the North because the oil companies had carved up the South. In Ghana, pretty much everywhere it could but always – always- away from the main cities."

"Out of sight?"

He nodded.

"Since the political failure of slavery, their method seems to have focused on anonymity at all costs."

Rushes of panic adrenaline saw me easily keep up with the autistic Ugandan now.

"They'd learnt the hard lesson the first time round."

"The owners of the original Royal African Company

included men like Sir Christopher Wren and Samuel Pepys and, of course, the monarchy. But within 150 years, the politicians had banned their most profitable venture. Maybe successive leaders of Royal Africa intended that they never again suffer such a fate."

"What's the significance of the dates of the purchases…"

I realised just after I'd asked.

"…Independence from British rule."

"My thought too, Mr Wright. They no longer owned the countries so needed to secure their profit before other interests could gain a hold."

We stopped for breath. One of the children had fallen off the climbing frame and its howls of panic were being ignored by the gang of mothers.

"And the rest, Viner, the bank?"

Okello perked up a bit, eager to show what he'd hacked and grabbed.

"It's all in the notebook, Mr Wright. Viner used to be spelt with a 'Y'. He was a seventeenth-century Lord Mayor of London, filthy rich, notable to us maybe because he kept a dead dried black child in a box to show dinner guests."

"You what?"

"He was a main player in the Royal African Company and frequent lender to the king."

"Frank. Can you go back a sentence, please?"

"The dried dead black child? Read Samuel Pepys' diaries, just go online. It's all there. You have to remember, Mr Wright, Samuel Pepys was a secret diarist. They were not intended to be read by anyone until after his death."

"So, our modern-day Viner?"

"Some shares in Royal African Holdings have passed down the generations. This Viner seems to have spent time in the British military, ending up with special forces. He spent a lot of it in Africa."

"Banque de Montagne?"

"Originally owned by a French-Swiss family with links to the City of London. Henri Chevalier is a direct descendant too. It now serves as the main network for Royal Africa to move funds about the world."

I leaned back into the uncomfortable park bench trying to ground myself, eyes wide like a religious zealot seeing the true Satan for the first time. The child had stopped screaming and was munching on a pacifying snack. Okello continued my re-education, his tone as unemotional as if he were describing a brand of toilet cleaner.

"Cubbins, Jacques and Heward was formed from two mergers many decades ago. Cecil Jacques was Banque de Montagne's main legal adviser. John Cubbins was actually an original shareholder in the seventeenth-century Royal African venture and the firm is today Royal Africa's main lawyer. It appears that Heward had strong links across many former British colonies. Your Mr Taylor is actually the partner in charge of so-called 'special relations' there. He has a surprisingly light digital footprint, which is often the profile of someone employed by the security services."

I noticed heavy sweat, squeezed from the polluted stew of a London summer day, trickle down into the crack of my arse. The munching child had recovered and was now back whacking another infant with a stick.

"And the final piece – our young Nigerian friend?"

"Ah yes. Folusha Danjuma, known to friends as 'Flo'. He's the twelfth official son of a well-known general, now deceased. Educated, as were his siblings, at English boarding schools and then on to good universities…"

"Salaries for Nigerian generals are higher than anywhere else in the world by quite a long way."

"A great pity for their country. Danjuma now works as a private client fund manager looking after a part of the fortunes of a dozen rich families, but his biggest client by far is Captain Robert Viner. Maybe Royal Africa Capital decided some time ago it needed more people with local contacts for when things went wrong. It's a best guess only."

Frank Okello's guess was as educated as a Harvard emeritus. The brilliant man finished and waited for any further instruction. He seemed to have taken only minor satisfaction from exposing the full extent of his prowess.

Things slipped inwards for me. The Royal African Company, the weight of corrupted summer heat pressing into my lungs. It was how the last person left outside might feel when the globally warmed planet had had its way with humanity.

"How hard was this all to find, Frank?"

"I have been running searches, breeches, covers and applied some deductive reasoning since you texted me two days ago."

"Any chance they spotted you? I guess you know from what you've told me that we could be gone quickly if these people wanted it."

Okello scratched his leg, considering the answer, the closest I had ever seen to a tell. He wasn't greatly capable of lying.

"There is always a risk, Mr Wright, but I would say it is quite low. Private banks and law firms don't hire anywhere near the top of the gene pool in my area."

'Quite low' and that leg scratch opened up chasms of anxiety.

"Did you find anything about Yaw Asante? Some big men took him away in a green Mercedes according to his neighbour."

"No, which isn't surprising. But strangely less and less on Lawrence Michaels too. It's as if they both have been erased from the digital landscape, but in Michaels' case, it's a bit slower. His debts are being paid off and affairs run down by someone."

We sat for a while then I sighed loudly, the noise of someone lifting twice their body weight for the first time.

"Frank, this is all problematic."

"Yes, I agree, Mr Wright. You need to be careful."

The Ugandan rose steadily, then jerked his way out of the green. I watched him, wondering if it was the meds that did that. The story he'd told me would no doubt sign his ticket back into the mental institution from which I had rescued him, and in that moment, I truly wished it so. I pleaded with myself to believe that his compromised imagination had concocted the whole fantasy, etching it all faithfully into a small book of madness that I could then hand over to the appropriate authorities. I wished. My fear wished. And then the wishing turned to fatigue as terror percolated into me, roughing up invisible edges until they grazed my insides raw. I texted Kate.

Hey, darlin', just checking we are meeting tomorrow. It's Friday and I know you gonna need some after a hard week climbing the corporate pole.

The exhaustion rapidly returned like a trench man in the First World War after the shelling had stopped for the night. The flames of Frank Okello's story had burnt through my essential fabric, leaving barely enough material to bother carrying on. After a long while spent just concentrating on breathing, I summoned the will to call Kobi with a plan for the evening ahead.

11

THURSDAY EVENING

Kate's smiling emoji reply pinged as I entered the shop off Brick Lane, which sold fashion pieces to women working a few yards and a world away in the City of London.

Yiolanda, my old school friend and the sometimes wife of my fantasies, was both the owner and today the sales assistant of her Bishopsgate emporium, Flava Chic. She raised a well-kept eyebrow under a lovely head wrap as I shambled through the door.

My dissolving smile lacked all conviction. This was a long way from going with my best foot.

"Just in the area so thought would drop by."

She apologised with her hands then walked towards her store room to take a call. I tried to gather my dishevelled self up into something more palatable. Deliveries arranged, Yiolanda returned looking concerned. Maybe I looked like I felt.

"Nice stuff you got here."

"Yes it is." She stroked the arm of a denim jacket into which had been expertly woven intricate shimmering onyx sequins.

"We get them from all over Africa and here too, of course. You'd be amazed how many talented black designers there are in the UK still looking for a route to market. The more mainstream shops won't have 'em."

"One of your many competitive advantages then?"

That received a knowing nod. I didn't appreciate small talk any more than she, but I did like to understand business.

"What's going on with you?" Yiolanda's worry was vaulting far above the question she'd calmly asked.

"Oh. Working two cases at the moment – long hours."

"What you do sounds difficult. I imagine it sometimes gets complicated."

"Piecing things together at the moment." I avoided her eyes lest she see the fear oozing from them and mistake it for something like a sickness of the mind.

"I might be going to Ghana in the next few days to chase down a lead."

Her eyes lit up, rising suns framed by the peaks of those beautiful high cheekbones.

"Really? Lucky you. I haven't been for two years! Got your visa?"

"Don't need one. Renewed the Nigerian passport my dad got me before he cut out."

"Well, if you do go, please say. I have friends there, could put you up. I'll tell them to treat you just perfectly!"

'Just perfectly'. My inner voice cried out for the person who would do that.

"Gotta go, Yiolanda. Good to see you. Will be in touch for that coffee."

She stepped forward to kiss my cheek then pulled back as if her approach had been thwarted by some repulsive force emitted by the nearly dead to stop others being taken with them to nothingness. She offered questioning eyes, trying to figure out what was happening, and it took effort for me to hide from them.

"Take care of yourself, Joseph."

Outside the bubble of failed potential that the shop represented, the evening's tasks re-formed into view. Kobi was already in place. When he realised we weren't coming, Barker would walk towards Liverpool Street station to feed his pole-dancer addiction or to take the underground train back to his wife. We held clear advantages on the currency trader. We knew his face, his address, and he didn't ours. He was over-confident. Most importantly, when it came to issues of violence, there was the Kobi factor.

I ordered, then sat slumped outside a patisserie in Spitalfields Square, scanning passing figures behind sunglasses, sipping a fragrant tea to soothe my tremors. Kobi messaged at 7:28.

Big Man on his way to you – he has interesting friends.
I pressed delete.

The man who came into view was not what you would have expected from his pictures – a short unfit frame in a cheaper-than-average grey suit. He was walking as quickly as his small legs could carry him, talking in some agitation to the two far-larger companions at his side. These were more in line with what I had imagined: close-cut, thick-necked men, wearing violence like some kind of bad aftershave. Despite the heat, both sported bomber jackets zipped at the waist under which a wide array of weapons might be kept for easy access. The way they nodded grimly at the end of each of his outbursts made the short commander boss.

I looked down and texted Kobi.

Let's follow the henchmen – we got Big Man sorted already.

The men saw their leader off at the east entrance to the train station. A text flew in.

I'll take the large geezer just in case.

Kobi was shorter than me, neither heavily muscled nor thickly built, but, still, he was as right as a judge before sentencing.

The smaller thug took a bus east, past Mile End and the uncomfortable newness of stadia built to host an Olympic Games whose hope had vanished as quickly as a politician's soundbite. I stationed myself meekly on the ground floor, waiting for the man to descend from the first, and followed him home at a distance.

I knocked on his front door thirty minutes later

because there wasn't a bell. A prematurely middle-ageing woman opened up.

"Yeah. Wot you want?" The way she emphasised 'you' told me a fair amount of what needed to be understood.

"Delivery?"

She turned, shouting back up the stairs.

"Jason, you ordered a pizza?"

"No. Tell him he's got the wrong 'ouse!"

I gesticulated an apology with the pizza box I'd just purchased up the road and used more than a hint of a Nigerian accent to prod her anger a bit more.

"Oh, sorry, boss. Think I have mistaken the postcode." The woman shook her head in disgust, muttering something under her breath about 'fucking immigrants' as she slammed the door.

By the time I took the overground to where Kobi was waiting, night was threatening to strangle the summer evening. I arrived as day was gasping its last wisps of life. Kobi was seated dead still under a small tree fifty metres from a near-derelict-looking pub. His wolf spirit was starting to merge with the night. It fed him and willed that he offer up sacrifices to its power. He gazed up as if in mediation with it, then nodded at the flags of St George hanging proudly on the windows of the establishment to which his prey had retired after the disappointing postponement of some promised violence.

"See what we are looking at here?" Kobi's eyes shone like gun metal in the shadow of his bench.

"A firm of hooligans with maybe a dash of old-fashioned racism thrown into the mix."

He hissed a short laugh at my description.

"There are plenty of black ones too now."

"Doesn't make these the United Nations."

"You know what I was saying earlier about people not letting me be myself?"

"Was thinking about it on the way over here. I just try not to fall into the cartoon role that this country seems to want to assign for me. But the pull is strong; it's always lurking somewhere like the cat in *Tom and Jerry*."

"That makes the real you the cartoon mouse, Jo." My mouth creased at the truth of the thing. Kobi was as calm as a priest at a deathbed.

"They have those roles too, you know. Different from ours but the same. Take this fellow here. Which dumb heavy in which shit movie do you think he thinks he is?"

"What shall I do with him?"

I knew the man by my side well enough to know he wasn't really asking. He would go wherever the night spirit led. I told him what I needed and let him decide.

"Follow him home, get his address and anything else that you can."

At this moment 130 kilograms of drunken rhinoceros tumbled out of the pub a little less purposefully than I imagined he had gone in. He whipped unsteadily round to peer back inside for a second before heading off towards bed.

"How about we mug him, take his wallet and see? He won't know it was anything to do with earlier – just two more wogs to be hated."

"Risky. You'd end up having to hit that thick head quite hard, Kobi, which might kill him there and then. If he survives, he'll likely get straight up and go take revenge on some youth somewhere."

"Yes. Probably."

I knew Kobi didn't give two shits about the beating some poor child might take, but he did seem to have considered a related issue.

"How about…" He paused. The night breathed more of its potency into him.

"I have a place, you know, Jolene. Where we could take him and get some answers. It's a lockup just outside London – very remote. We could grab a car, put him in the boot – be there in no time without traffic."

The fever from earlier on Newington Green returned instantly. My eyes widened enough to break the socket bone, my hands petrified in spasm in the presence of a pure evil that was revealing itself fully to me for the first time. I rooted them to the tops of my thighs to stop me trying to strangle either him or myself simply out of fear.

The wolf Kobi could smell blood in the lies of others, which wasn't safe for the liar, so I gave him what I had as straight as I could bring it.

"If you want someone to torture, that's fine, bro.

But I still need to know the size of the firm, who they are and if Wade Barker is top dog."

Kobi sat for a few seconds more. The receding outline of the bulky catch he was planning to devour meant a decision had to be made quickly.

"OK, Jolene, maybe your way. I'll text with the information."

He got up with almost superhuman speed, then started walking somehow both casually and rapidly in the direction of his drunken victim, fading quickly out of sight like some fairy-tale demon. I fingered a number, got no pickup then rang my Nigerian client for an update and was put through to the most well-spoken voicemail message I'd ever heard.

Hello, this is Olatunde Folarin. My apologies but I am on duty at the moment so please leave a message and I will reply tomorrow morning.

I caught myself grinning at the formality of the man, then laughed out loud and heartily like some ranting drunkard. The day had taken a lot. I could've gratefully given in to sleep right away on the softness of the mossy bench but dragged my forsaken body to the minicab office opposite Camden station and slept on the back seat on the hour-long drive to Peckham Rye.

12

FRIDAY

"**M**r Folarin." I checked myself, wondering why I'd started calling him 'Mr'.

It was 6am and he was on the way home from the night security shift he worked at Cubbins, Jacques and Heward. He didn't sound tired though.

"Mr Wright."

I gazed out at the light blue of a morning sky, still unstained with the suffering of those who would soon wake to live under it.

"Things have moved. I am heading to Accra tomorrow to chase them up."

He was shocked but tried not to let on.

"Moved how? Is Yaw OK?"

The answer didn't need to be born yet.

"It seems Asante is involved with people who value money a great deal more than an African life. I need to find out what I can to try and help."

I guessed the man at the end of the phone was getting on a bus, which had diluted the intended power of my words.

"I have purchased a British Airways ticket – seven hundred pounds as last minute. Thought you should know."

"I only have five hundred more for this, Joseph, and that is stretching it."

"Understood. I will contact you by next Saturday. I need to impress upon you now, Mr Folarin, do not discuss this matter with anyone. We are in a dangerous situation."

It was a good bet that a man who'd spent a career in the Nigerian civil service had seen his fair share of corrupted power.

"Now it is my turn to say 'understood', Joseph."

I punched the off sign, then sent Kate a picture of my cock in case she was considering not turning up in the evening.

The cushioned plastic throne hugged my buttocks, and I noticed how good I felt for a man one misstep away from torture and death. It was optimism of a sort but then this pitiful flavour could easily have been the chemical result of the previous night's drinking holiday than anything more real.

I would have gone to Ghana whether Folarin had paid or not. Yaw Asante was likely cold dead somewhere; the fate of any African who chose to gatecrash a money-printing machine uninvited.

I wasn't traveling there for him at all. We had been careful, but our measure of care was only meaningful in relation to an everyday adversary. We hadn't known what we were going against and wouldn't have started if we had.

The trauma of Royal Africa's footprint had stamped down the generations, seared into the unconscious of those who might draw its anger. And its existence confirmed, it had torn through the bones of a young black man, left him shitting his pants in abject panic as the beast walked about above him searching. Sleep had helped me come to terms with our chances, but anything that could raise them just slightly was like oxygen out on a Martian plain.

My mobile rang with the standard chime. I knew people who'd been identified simply by their unusual ringtone.

"Joseph Wright. What the fuck do you want!"

"Hello, Cushnie."

For some reason, I wasn't frightened of the distributor of illegal product, which put me in a minority of one. It was partly because I'd known him ten years back when he was still a teenager donning balaclavas for stupid night-time suburban break-ins. Partly also that I felt he relied on a weakness I didn't possess: people's need to belong to something; for kinship, a group to witness a life otherwise invisible to the universe.

"Why the call last night, Joseph? Remember the rule we had last time we dealt?"

Cushnie had hired me to find something on a prison guard committed to ruining the already-unpleasant experience of one of his gang who'd gone down for not ratting him out. The man possessed few obvious weaknesses. There were no parents alive, no siblings, partner or children. He seemed to live purely for the job of breaking those entrusted to his care. I had spent a few days scratching my head until I realised the answer was staring me in the face. I found him cruising a bar in South Kensington, then hired an underage-looking male prostitute to entrap him, dropping off the standard photo album at his flat only two days after the revelation had hit me. The threat of being labelled a nonce, coupled with the bigotry of his prison guard colleagues, was more than enough to settle the issue. He instantly became as malleable as fine porcelain clay and Cushnie gained a useful minion on the inside.

When the criminal intermediary offered me a job in lieu of payment for my wonderful work, I argued that a guy like me would be more valuable to him on the outside looking in as long as we could occasionally trade favours. The lean black male model, descended from the enslaved and determined to die before accepting any hint of that fate for himself, looked at me tungsten hard, wondering if he should simply remove the discomfort I had caused. He wasn't used to counter-argument but finally agreed with a condition.

"Remember, Joseph, you never wanna go into deficit with me. Not for long."

"I need to buy a glue gun, Cushnie. A small tool for close-up work and a pack of refills."

"You getting into something. Round my area?"

Cushnie could at any time be the subject of a significant police surveillance operation but I had to take the risk.

"A job's getting a bit more tricky than I first thought, though its nowhere near you."

"When do you need it?"

"As soon as."

"Be here after midnight."

Out in the park, the morning regulars were toiling on their various ways up the fitness mountain. I did a couple of circuits at seventeen kilometres per hour to sweat some of the worry out and was deciding whether to do a third when an email tinged in from Kobi. It was a list of names, twenty-one in all. Some had addresses next to them, some not, others had names of wives and children. Then came a text message.

Big Man, with an emoji of a top hat and a dog.

I wandered distractedly back to my flat considering what cost might ultimately be paid for having a relationship with a serial killer of white men. But then that wasn't even close to my biggest problem.

The baptism of a shower was followed by a brief check on Ashley, who sounded high, then lastly, a message to Wade Barker to see how he responded to being slapped around a bit.

If you mess with us again, you will regret it.

The rush of power this brought jettisoned itself as quickly as it had arrived because delusions like that would get me killed faster than a teenage infantryman at the Battle of the Somme.

Kate sent a picture of her mouth in reply to my previous message. She hadn't gotten to work quite yet.

It is true that life moves into a finer focus when its precious existence is undermined. In the few hours with nothing else pressing at the seams, I became aware of this heightened state and how it might be used. My mind soared vertically, examining the problem from cloud height then down in a kamikaze dive at it, getting closer and closer until I could see the whites of those terrified sailors' eyes. I pulled up again, repeating the mental act until intuition formed into a plan.

I t felt a long journey back to Knightsbridge travelling through images of poverty more fitting for a lower-income nation and then finally arriving at an enclave firmly committed to denying awareness that any of that existed in Britain.

Denial might have been one reason Flo Danjuma's

flat was equipped with a below-par suite of security measures. Broad daylight was not so risky. An observant neighbour would easily assume this was a friend of the black fellow next door. I sneered at the inadequate lock as it gave quickly. On my instruction, Frank Okello had invaded Flo's home computer and found an orderly list of passwords stored carefully in one file. All the idiot's gates dependent on accessing just one. I fingered the stolen code into an alarm pad, entered the main ground-floor living area through a narrow hall then sat on Danjuma's sofa, savouring the feeling of taking him this way.

Mews houses were originally built as stables to keep the horses of the aristocracy. This thoroughbred certainly lived better than the donkeys in my tower block, but, still, I was disappointed by the cheapness of the Nordic DIY furniture. I carefully moved around the room, snapping pictures of anything that looked useful or simply out of place. Jammed into cheap frames lay three photos – the only ones in house. These were placed on the mid-section of a slightly wonky shelving unit which had once maintained aspirations to be the poor cousin of some mid-twentieth-century European design movement.

The largest depicted my prey's boarding school rugby team. Flo stood near the centre, surrounded by a jostling group of teenagers, a physical peak of the separate species that was economic privilege.

Next to it was a picture of a young woman in

traditional Nigerian dress, probably at a wedding. She posed like some minor deity of African mythology, holding the hand of her small boy child who would soon be sent away to Britain at a devastatingly early age. Her eyes refused to engage the camera, which nonetheless captured something of the melancholy that a girl might feel as the fifth wife of a man old enough to be her grandfather.

Peering closer at the third picture, I spotted a member of the rugby team, now ten years older, out on the town, his arm around Flo, smiling his Ghanaian smile, the joy of the moment amplified somehow by the lustre of expensive tastes. Written in fluid fountain-pen stroke in the cream border of the photograph:

JT–FD brothers for life!

Up narrow stairs, I invaded the one small bedroom that the house had to offer. The contents of the Nigerian money manager's clothes collection contrasted sharply with the white veneer and plastic units that housed them. Here were pieces – jackets, jeans, trousers – that cost multiples of the yearly income of the average London worker. I rifled through silk-lined pockets and linen sleeves, ending up with a single business card.

Windsor Corporate Finance, Airport, Accra. John (Toks) Owusu. JT.

Located behind and below the trousers sat a large shallow safe, whose combination had been stupidly left with all the other passwords. I groped its insides, croupier fingers sifting quickly but methodically through the man's secrets.

There were a few mementos of conquest: nude stills of girls who'd agreed to compromise themselves in various ways. Under these, a picture of Flo's serious father bursting pompously out of a tight military uniform. Then a thin ring-binder file marked strangely with some kind of symbol, which resembled a four-leaf clover. Inside were copies of official-looking documents, some of which matched those I had snapped in the Croydon pastor's office. At the back lay the name of the Accra land registry officer who'd overseen the processing of the paperwork – Mr Kwame Opoku-Brown.

I went downstairs with one of the nude photos and masturbated into Flo's guest toilet. Afterwards, I made sure all was as I'd found it.

The number thirty-six bus took over an hour to crawl its way from the crown of London's tree to its roots below ground. I stared outwards with the gaze of the dying taking in scenes that looked more real, colours that emitted themselves more deeply. Had Yaw Asante felt the same on his final Mercedes-driven ride? And I saw how it could all have been worth the risk for Asante, a man so nearly invisible in Britain that his disappearance had been noticed by only one person. Those papers and the money they promised were not only a path back to Ghana, but they also represented a way to regain form in the world.

A text came in from the woman who might have been the mother to my seven-year-old child had fate offered a different menu.

Your man visits Beryl Roberts every fourth Monday evening between 8pm and 9pm. Next visit not due for two weeks. She sees clients in a room above the Golden Arch Indian restaurant off Brick Lane. Goodbye, Joseph.

Walking home from the bus stop, I clicked on a reply from the sex-addicted banker who I was hoping to beat or blackmail into stopping persecuting Global Banking Corporation's first black trainee currency trader.

Alright. Let's do it your way.

He still wasn't scared.

13

FRIDAY EVENING

Kate rang the bell because she didn't have a key. I opened the door in boxer shorts and a gown, and she immediately glanced down to see if my welcoming committee was up and ready. There was no erection-to-order and I gestured in the style of a gallant gentleman towards the living room and balcony.

She seemed a touch heavier than I'd seen her ten days ago, the silky brown hair less well-tended, and her skin was red in places where insufficient sun block had been applied in search of a faster tan. I poured her a cognac to meet my own and she produced some papers to roll up the weed she'd brought. We sat out on the balcony and tried to loosen away the knots of a failed relationship with the caresses of the drugs we each relied upon to get through this life.

"Seems like a long time, Kate – longer than usual."

"Yeah – work, I guess." She casually exhaled a big cloud of weed upwards, which I ducked because it had never agreed with me.

"How's it going over there?"

Kate always seemed reluctant to discuss the minutia of the small branch office in which she toiled, as if exposing her day world to my twilight one might somehow undermine its validity.

"Ugh, don't ask! Targets and more targets from above but who the hell really knows whether a customer is gonna bite or not? Sales guys getting really stressed; market activity is in the doldrums."

"That's because house prices in London are too expensive for most people to afford."

"Maybe, but the sellers won't come down apart from the people cashing in when their parents have kicked the bucket."

"People are usually worth more dead now than when they're alive." I thought of Asante, whose life had been valued at close to zero, alive or not.

Kate put out the end of her joint, reclining invitingly in the chair, feet on the table, legs apart. It had been two weeks and I didn't need a second invitation.

Later, I ordered a takeaway with all the trimmings.

"Where do you get your money from, Joseph?"

"I told you, I'm a big drug dealer, babe."

She smiled but wasn't going to be thwarted by sarcasm.

"You never seem short, never stressed by it. There won't be anyone living around 'ere that can say that. There's not anyone I work wiv can either."

The question was as broad as could be. She was asking about my life and our future. We'd been together a year and she knew so little about my day to day. How much would I give her?

I regarded the steady creep of cellulite on the backs of her thighs, the thickening of a waistline, all now important somehow. A shot of cognac hit the back of the throat, diffusing into my brain like a comfort blanket.

"Let's see. I'm on a job at the moment where a man has disappeared. People who disappear like he has have usually been murdered by somebody, which means there are killers involved. On this second job, a violent lunatic is trying to lure me into meeting so he and his boys can do me some serious harm."

Kate wasn't really listening. My explanation was being drowned out by the shouts of her own internal reactions. It could've been the weed or maybe I just wasn't giving what she needed.

"The reason I am saying this, Kate, apart from to get it off my chest, is that there are risks. Risks that most people either won't take or if they do, get quickly found out. Like many men my colour in this country, I am actually underpaid for what I do but sometimes there's a lot of dough in it."

She curled her still-youthful body onto all fours,

crawling towards me on the bed, which became a hug. That hug automatically brought forth more feelings.

"If I'd had access to your economic system, I might not be doing this at all. I might be a lawyer or the best estate agent in South London. I don't know – parents, me, the system – it didn't go that way and this is where I'm at."

I tried to lighten the weight that was dragging our relationship down to its inevitable ending.

"Plus, you gotta remember this flat is practically rent free given it's still in crazy fucking Mum's name."

The food arrived and we ate greedily, Kate because of the effects of the weed. It was my first meal of the day. We watched some episodes of her favourite TV show, which involved some youngish white people engaging the various trials and tribulations of their world, armed mainly with a light-hearted camaraderie. Kate's head nestled sleepily in my lap.

At about 11:30pm, I rose to shower.

"I gotta go out for an hour or two now, babes."

She woke from the dream as if she'd been stabbed in the meat of her thigh.

"Out? What? But…"

"It's to do with the cases I told you about. I won't be long."

"When were you intending to tell me this and… who the fuck goes out at midnight, Joseph? What for?"

"I've got to see someone who will have something for me."

She was shaking her head, anger building with the hurt of abandonment and betrayal of misinformation.

"Something. What thing, Jo? Please tell?"

"Information. It's unfortunate but it is a matter of life and death." My own life and death, but what was the point of saying? Could she really comprehend it?

Kate got the rest of herself off me, primed with emotional violence, weapons warming up to unload. She looked in my eyes, searching for the hook upon which to launch her first grenades, but they were dead. I gave up nothing, by instinct and training because I'd been here a million times before from as early as I could remember. She slumped back onto the sofa in abject confusion.

"How do you expect us to have anything like this, Jo?"

She could tell I didn't care. I didn't even say goodbye after I'd showered and withdrawn the bundle of cash kept under a faded picture of my father wearing a shoulder-padded suit from the '80s.

14

SATURDAY, 12AM

As far I could remember, Cushnie had always lived in a desolate corner of South East London, down a road going nowhere in what had been a set of garages situated behind a forlorn row of permanently failing shops. He'd expanded over the years from the one converted unit to all eight, the owners having been given no option other than to agree to his proprietorship. I suspected he now owned most of the shops too.

The garages offered a compelling hierarchy of security. The first layer was simply the cover of anonymity. Cushnie might be the richest man in the borough, but he still lived amongst the poorest. More important, given how far he'd gotten in the game, were the physical advantages of the site. It was a small fortress. The garage units backed onto a thick retaining wall; the only access to them was through a narrow driveway, which he had heavily monitored. Behind eight rusty garage handles now stood steel barriers. A reinforced door sat at the furthest corner, the only entrance into the windowless steel concrete box.

Cushnie had at some point been the son of Caribbean immigrants who'd long ago disappeared from his life. I sometimes wondered at the interplay of traumatic ingredients that had constituted the earth that moulded him. He had dozens on the payroll but was usually only accompanied by two henchmen, Carl and Nick, lesser mortals but fashioned from a similar type of material. One of these, Carl, met me at the front barrier. There was no need for a bell.

"Jo."

We nodded. I was let into the first antechamber. A second bullet-proofed door was then unlocked by Nick and I was pointed down the red-lit hallway to the room at the rearmost point of the building.

Cushnie was sat on his expensive Italian leather sofa watching reruns of prime Roy Jones fights on a large TV screen. The man was a young Sydney Poitier, truly handsome under the disguise of a standard baseball cap. A scalpel-sharp mind had seen him prosper where thousands failed, a chess grandmaster in a game where the pieces were real people.

Tonight, he was with his long-term girlfriend, Lisa, a pale waif of a woman, who was vaguely aware of how terrified she was of him but too terrified to be that aware of it. She seemed to be consuming increasing amounts of weed each time I'd seen her to ward off the panics that living under constant threat might otherwise have produced.

We exchanged nods, then Cushnie gestured to a chair on the right of his Conran furniture.

"Sit down. Drink?" He didn't mean the second bit.

"Lisa." She flinched almost imperceptibly as he said her name. He noticed too and, I realised, liked it that way.

"Can you go to the other room for a while? Joseph and I need to have a chat."

Once the slave woman had done what she was told, her owner turned to me. His voice was soft, lacking intonation of emotion, which effectively conveyed an intended sense of menace.

"What you want the tool for?"

I knew he'd ask. I gave him the story of my second case – a firm of hooligans run by a City trader who was persecuting a young brother trying to make it in their world.

He could hear the truth in it all but, through a rare gift of intuition, sensed something was off and sat back to ponder what, eventually settling on the one aspect that didn't feel right.

"So… you need it in case they come at you?" My survival microscope spotted the problem quickly. Cushnie didn't regard this bunch of thugs as worthy of the weapon I had ordered. He also knew I had Kobi, a factor more lethal than any small firearm.

"There's something about them, Cushnie. Looking into it right now but am guessing former army – a few of 'em, at least. If that's the case, I don't want to be caught without. Those guys have all got PTSD from Afghanistan. They are fucking insane."

The youthful Caribbean King Solomon sat back again for some time unpicking my words, tracing the paths that came off them and others that might follow those. After a while, the air around him relaxed some.

"You know my name is Scottish, Jo?"

"Some randy plantation owner doing his ting three hundred years ago."

The rarest of animals, a Cushnie smile, briefly appeared.

"Yeah, but it means I am part of a clan. I've got a tartan and shit. I'm thinking of going up to visit them all one day in Scotland. My clan."

"Prodigal son. Am sure they'll be thrilled to see you."

The criminal-for-life brought out a sports bag from under the coffee table and, after checking inside, I handed over money. There was nothing else to say so he simply returned to watching the genius American boxer at work. I walked down the hallway, past the penultimate chamber where Lisa was watching the same TV show I'd seen earlier in the evening, waiting to return to the struggle for life that was her relationship.

Nick came out of his room to see me off. He had picked up a long thin scar under an eye and down a cheek since we'd last met. He hated me because he secretly suspected the job I'd been offered by Cushnie had been his. But the rottweiler of a man wouldn't do anything unless told to and that thought sustained me across the two barriers, out of the red light and into the freshness of night.

Kate was asleep when I got back – too late to leave, I guessed. I crept outside to my balcony sanctuary with the caution of someone who felt watched. The cool of the night was quickly losing the battle with utter exhaustion after adrenaline had done its precarious work at the gangster's residence. A dram of copper-gold spirit helped redress the balance long enough to send two final texts.

Tomorrow at 10:30pm. St George in the East Church. Tower Hamlets. This is the last chance to solve your problem, Barker. If you mess around you, will suffer.

I put aside stabbing prophecies of dread and sent a message to the best friend I'd ever had.

Hey, Kobi…

15

SATURDAY MORNING

By the time Kate woke up, I had been for a six-kilometre run and was seated outside overseeing my kingdom passing beneath. The day was born with many features of the night that had sired it. Northern winds had gifted a crispness, removing pollution that would otherwise be sticking to the skin by midday.

My girlfriend walked heavy-legged into the small functional living area that adjoined the balcony. She had a shyness this morning, perhaps remembering our last words, and I sat deciding whether to indulge it with tenderness. One look at Kate in a morning after some serious weed smoking and a hard work week settled things.

"I am going to Ghana tomorrow. Two, three days tops."

I didn't get up to hug her nor beckoned her on,

so she stood in the small living room framed by the orange Formica drawers of the kitchenette, caught in a no-woman's land of cheap 1980s furnishing. I almost laughed at the scene.

"What's funny, Jo?"

"What? Nothing. OK. Just your face when I told you I was off to Ghana."

"Was it a joke then – a snide way to throw me off somehow?"

"No, no. It's true. I am going, Kate. Not for a holiday, I promise you that."

Kate had wanted to go to the Canaries last summer but I'd fobbed her off saying I couldn't think of anything worse than hanging out with a group of South London estate agents and their other halves.

"Why then? You got a Ghanaian girl tucked away somewhere then, mate?"

"No. Unlike many African men you've ever heard of, I am not polyamorous, my love. It's just the case. The man that disappeared, the one I told you about last night. He comes from Ghana."

"I've always wanted to see Africa, Jo."

"Yes, and one day I am sure there'll be a nice safari just right for you."

She reeled at the verbal slap, turned quickly lest I see its effect, picked up a T-shirt from the sofa and stomped dejectedly to the bedroom. The mouse wheel of estate agency required employees to be in at 9am on Saturdays. Kate returned bravely to the living room twenty minutes later to say goodbye. She'd showered and brought different clothes, smart but more casual for the half-day stint. She looked beautiful and as straightforward as the evening we'd met. It triggered in me a flash of self-contempt. Why was I unable to put down the anger of the previous night and connect with this woman who gave me her body and asked the right questions?

"I'm going now, Jo."

It felt more like a question than a statement. She looked down at me with sadness.

"I feel sorry, Joseph, but not for me. I know what you do, you know, and I am one hundred per cent certain you are good at it. All the lying and manipulating. Peddling the secrets of desperate people. But where's your life, Jo? Where are your people?"

The truth of the words could easily have brought tearful wails at the loneliness her departure would bring, but the part that came to rescue my vulnerability wasn't caring or nourishing. It didn't say, *I love you and I'm sorry for last night, please call me.* That's all it would have taken. It couldn't because that part hadn't been born for tenderness or love but to defend a toddler caught in a war zone called home.

I offered the parting gift of a blank stare. She took it, shaking her head slightly, and left, slamming the front door as Ashley had done a few nights before. The day was sucking me forwards to who knew what, but before it did, I watched a miniature Kate cut across Peckham Rye and disappear into the trees.

My phone's message notifier provided the perfect cut-off between the failure of the past and worries of the future. It was Frank Okello.

Mr Wright, can we meet, 2pm today at the summit of Primrose Hill?

I sent the thumbs up. It gave me time. Enough to clean the firearm, scatter away the loss of a girlfriend and prepare for anything.

Primrose Hill reminded me of what life could have been were I born to be a successful actor, businessman or poet. The park's well-tended grounds were serenaded on the east by beautiful pastel-painted houses. To the north and west lay the spacious apartment buildings of the wealthy foreigners who chose to make London their home and then, at the southwestern border, London's only major zoo just on the doorstep.

Okello had chosen to stand and as I approached, he turned his head to regard me in the usual impassive android-like manner. Slanting sun rays diffused over his spectacles, hiding the little emotion his eyes might be offering.

"Hey, Frank. What you got for me?"

He gazed back out at the London skyline then pointed a straight arm at the financial district, whose herd of brutal skyscrapers looked like an army of gigantic automata ready to carry out the destructive will of some omnipotent master.

"Wade Barker is interesting."

"He's the head of a group of hooligans and likes prostitutes. Have you found anything about his team? Any armed forces in there?"

"Yes, three of them. I will forward the details."

"I'm flying to Accra tomorrow to follow up on Asante's disappearance."

"He's likely dead, Mr Wright."

"Yes, he is. Flo Danjuma has a friend called John Toks Owusu. Can you get his address in Accra?"

"I have it already. His number too." The eccentric Ugandan produced a small fold-up computer from a grey trench coat, closely caressing a few keys into sending an electronic stanza.

I felt an odd dizziness.

"Why are we here, Frank? You could have emailed me all of this already."

"I am worried, Mr Wright. Someone may be tracking me online. If so, they are top class and I told you these people wouldn't employ that type. I am sorry that I did not tread more carefully as you asked."

My mouth made a shape but couldn't manufacture the usual sound, so strangled out the minimum needed to persist with the conversation.

"What's the chances?"

"Over half. I have moved out. I don't think they've got you yet."

"Your sister?"

"She's in Kampala at the moment."

I noticed a knee starting to jitter violently. The newly acquired metal comforted me a touch but the tiny gun wouldn't keep death away for long if called into action against forces like these.

"Will try to get us something in Accra. You understand what this is, right, Frank?"

"I do. In fact, I've always worried that it existed, Mr Wright. Always. The inflicter of uncountable pains and injustices. Its birth came after the millennia of the Pharaohs." Something in Frank suggested real curiosity where fear should have stalked. He'd maybe had a whole lifetime to adjust to our present situation.

"The seed was already present when Rome ruled Britain. They called it Londinium. Twelve centuries later, it had matured, gaining form and influence. Then it metastasised, funding the annihilation of whole peoples in the Americas and the enslavement of millions more. It is the architect of history, Mr Wright."

"Architect, Frank?"

The fever of worry saw me struggle to look at the Ugandan programmer now.

"Yes. Most powers like this can't help but announce themselves to a trembling world. They build monuments and fight great battles. But this is different. You Nigerians have a good phrase. Four One Nine. You could call hiding itself this way, the biggest Four One Nine in human history."

I nodded like a child on his first day at secondary school.

"Once I have secured my operation, I will be in touch."

Okello turned sharply, his movement now assured as if the proximity of danger was stripping away jerky affectations he'd developed simply for fun.

"You need a new mobile, Mr Wright."

He jogged quickly down the hill to a small white van, got in and sped off. I didn't even know he could drive.

The terror of being out in the open forced itself onto me. Royal Africa had special forces deployed by software surveillance capabilities that even Frank admired. There had to be a place to rest, to undertake the emotional bookkeeping required to stumble on. I started running, picked up a new phone from a small Camden repair shop, then moved rapidly south through places and streets that the millions of tourists, only five minutes away, were lucky never to see. I jostled down some stairs to the basement level of a nearly demolished-looking Georgian house that had somehow avoided that fate at the hands of the twentieth century's social housing planners. Rita, the tired brothel manager I had been unable to save from her sadistic client, answered the door. Her contempt hadn't lessened in the intervening years.

"Hmm. The useless detective."

"Hi, Rita. I am looking to have a good time and thought of you."

The small red-haired bordello owner didn't really believe me, but money was money.

"All my staff are busy right now. Come back in an hour."

"I can wait, Rita."

As I assumed the role of a punter, the woman's face transformed into the emotional equivalent of a black hole. Her chosen profession required it. Shows of emotion were risky because anything could trigger a client's shame, fear and then anger. I was led silently down into the small basement reception and quickly made a home in its tattered fake-leather couch. The room smelled strongly of stale cigarettes at the hands of the men whose daytime lives had been stubbed out in overflowing metal ashtrays. I lay back gratefully in the sanctuary of the squalor and let thoughts wander until they were aspiring to become dreams.

After about half an hour, a large middle-aged man came in wearing only boxer shorts, socks and some headgear. The pink around his eyes stood out against the rubber of the black domination mask he paid to put on here. He was brandishing a feather duster and set about cleaning the room around me. Rita followed holding a long lead, which I realised was attached to the back of the man's head.

"Minion, do some more cleaning!"

The brothel owner was so accustomed to playing the role that she sounded bored, but being hardly deserving of her insults somehow added to the buzz he got from the thing. The large man jiggled around the small room, diligently using the cleaning implement, ignoring me as if I was a piece of furniture, all the while being regaled with demeaning lashes from Rita's acid tongue.

"Minion. You are a pointless piece of dirt. You're not even worthy to lick my toilet."

The submissive carried on dutifully, feasting on the torrent of abuse, and then, in a moment of inspiration, Rita decided to bring me into the fantasy.

"You see that black man there. You aren't worthy to clean even his boots." The exposed stomach fat stopped wobbling at my head's height as its owner waited for instruction.

"Go on then. Offer him a cigarette and light it if he wants one."

He lumbered forward. I shook my head at the three cylinders of tobacco that were tapped out of the packet and she yanked at his umbilical lead.

"See, he doesn't want one from you! You can't even do that properly. You pathetic scum."

The couple wandered out of the door and I heard the insults lead them upstairs back to a bedroom. It was easy money for Rita unless his kink sought out more sinister pathways later into the fantasy.

A young woman with light-brown skin arrived soon after, taking me by the hand up to her room. The studio was a poorly lit ground-floor affair with hardly any space beyond a ragged double bed. A small sink stood in the corner next to a wardrobe lacking a door, which held under-sized plastic pink and green coat hangers. She looked at me timidly, half expecting some lecture on morals from her brother in mixed-race. I felt her story even if I didn't know it – not so far from my own with the odd embellishment of sexual abuse by a step-parent or uncle.

"Hi, I'm Jo."

"Ruth," she said, relaxing from the empathy she'd found in me.

"Listen, I just need a place to lie down."

"It's a hundred quid an hour." Her anxiety had shot to ceiling height. She didn't believe that I didn't desire her services and a customer racked with that kind of guilt was dangerous. I handed over the cash in fifties. The notes were snapped swiftly and inspected in the dull light of the one window that wasn't boarded from the outside.

"Listen, Rita knows me. I did work for her some time back."

She removed my trainers but nothing else. I stretched on the spongey mattress and made the deep escape of sleep an immediate destination.

I recoiled in panic as she woke me later. There was a tenderness in her touch – she did believe me now.

"What you got that gun for?"

The reality of my situation piled back into focus. I was a small-time crook in mortal danger from those far above me, hiding in a filthy backstreet brothel from God knew what. I felt so lost that I wanted to put my head on her chest and weep.

"It's – it's mainly for comfort, not for use."

"Why not get a cushion instead then?"

The joke lightened things enough for me to notice.

"You from Liverpool?"

"Good spot. You know it?"

"Did some stuff up there four years ago."

"You paid three hours. You've got one left. I just wanted to check that sleep was all you wanted to do."

I looked at the lovely young woman's curvy brown figure under the gossamer material of her bed gown. She registered the desire in those eyes, had seen it a thousand times.

"No, but I could do with another hour more."

She appreciated my self-control. Men usually visited to let loose the wild dogs of their failed lives, to make up for the shame of it in those few minutes of power that they might extract from her.

"Where do your parents come from, Ruth?"

"Dad's Jamaican, Mum's English."

"I'm half Nigerian, half English."

"Oh. I always wanted to go to Africa. Just to see, you know."

"One day then."

"My boyfriend's constantly talking about sliding back to Jamaica. Says he just feels better there."

"Does he know what you do for a living?"

"No, he's still up north. Think's I'm a receptionist trying to get some money for our first mortgage. I want to tell him, but I don't know how he'd take it."

"Don't then, Ruth. What's the point in risking it?"

"Because I want to have an honest relationship with him and I can't unless he knows. If you don't show at least one person everything, you end up very lonely."

I was struggling to come to terms with this revelation when Rita knocked on the door, then entered, having jettisoned her client face.

"Joseph, I am worried." Although she'd been raised here, there remained the Eastern European hint of her parents' upbringing, especially when she was nervous.

"It's OK. Give me ninety minutes and I'll be gone for good, Rita."

"Shit. I knew I shouldn't have used you. I am running a nice operation here now. You hear what I mean?"

I felt the threat behind Rita's words and considered what aces she must now be holding to issue it against a man like me. Maybe she'd gotten that protection after all.

"Ninety minutes. I'll pay and I will be gone."

She erred, gave a faint nod, then closed the door.

"See – she does know me!" I said to my new friend.

The wise young woman gave out a sagging smile as if she'd met men like this all her life and had the tarot cards of my future laid out in plain sight.

16

SATURDAY EVENING

Kobi was enjoying a joint in the grounds of St Botolph's-without-Bishopsgate Church, one of the only patches of grass surviving in a concrete-metal landscape that made up the Liverpool Street station area of the City of London.

On weekdays, the small gardens offered a lunchtime refuge to armies of City workers, escaping the precocious intrigues that formed the daily diet of survival for a career in finance. I perched on a bench behind a deck of trees bordering the small sanctuary that was also used at night by people without anywhere else to go. Kobi slid onto a bench two trees down greeting me with my lower-ranked moniker.

"Jolene."

"Hey, Kobs. This church was named after St Botwulf, the seventh-century patron saint of boundaries. That's because it sat just by the walls demarcating those living inside with all the money and everyone else trying to get in."

"You and your history books, J. Insiders and outsiders though."

Kobi was probably the only person alive who would have guessed where I was going with this thought.

"You know which side we're on, bro, and which they are on. If we get caught, we're done."

My friend was wearing his burglary outfit – black trainers and joggers and a dark baggy hooded jumper, which effectively concealed a large internal pocket for carrying. We both sported regulation baseball caps and looked down for the cameras as instinctively as birds fly south for the winter.

I rose first, taking the sharp right, then doubling back the other way round the train station so Kobi, who'd headed left, could then trail me at a distance for a few minutes to the lookout point I marked for him. We were over three hours early, but circumstances warranted a paranoia, which came naturally to us both. Barker still didn't have our faces and we wouldn't give that advantage up easily. Once Kobi was set in place, I mowed through narrow backstreets at speed, within a minute crossing from the universe of global finance into the parallel realm of Whitechapel's Bengali business community. Dozens of shops offered goods from clothing to food, at prices that customers on this side of the boundary might just be able to afford.

There followed a right turn at the hospital, the summer-evening chill lending a welcome crispness to mind and an agile sharpness to body. Now on my chosen street, I passed by several versions of housing that the twentieth century had invented for many. These cheap boxes bordered a glorious white church, built nearly three hundred years earlier by an understudy of one of the original shareholders of the Royal African slave-trading monopoly that was now probably trying to kill me. Frank was right. When you looked only a little, you realised they had been ever-present, in a country buckled to their will across centuries.

I stopped trembling now, a hundred metres from the beautiful church, and waited in an ageing Victorian railway tunnel, barely visible as the darkening blot of night extended itself from the shadows.

Two hours or so later, Kobi's text wafted into sight.

Big Man spotted. This time with twelve friends all in the advance party.

From their starting point, Barker's men had been sent forward to the grounds of the church to deal with us before he arrived. They weren't early, didn't feel the need for any advantage beyond overwhelming force. Maybe, in some warped fantasy, he wanted to be the one to strike a final blow to my head or simply stand enjoying the whines as I begged for my life. I exited the tunnel, crouching near its mouth behind one of the estates' communal rubbish sheds. Within a few heartbeats, Kobi had slipped silently behind me.

Minutes later, the crew marched past on the other side of the street, not more than ten metres away from us. They ranged greatly in size and shape but all maintained close-cut shaves and were carrying under accommodating jackets. Some strode confidently, faces fixed with the glue of determination. Other members of the platoon seemed to live for the rapture of these moments with the hunting pack, a grim joy etched on their features as they stomped out a meditative calm before the coming violence.

We had been prepared to tackle two or three others, but Barker was so confident he'd not kept any back for protection. What was about to happen simply hadn't occurred to him as he travelled purposefully into the tunnel. Kobi sprang from darkness, smashing the back of the man's head with a small wooden club. The boss hooligan collapsed limply, either dead or unconscious. We carried his body quickly to a van we had waiting by the south exit of the tunnel. There were no security cameras here; any witnesses in the surrounding tower blocks probably knew enough to keep to themselves, but, really, what could they see? A human being taken by the shadows. It lasted under sixty seconds in all and then it was like we'd never been there at all.

K obi took small narrow streets behind crumbling dwellings of Shoreditch, which bordered the City of London. After five minutes, he stopped north in a secluded square of the wealthy district of Islington to allow me to replace number plates.

The roll of the vehicle eventually rocked the little man awake. He started groaning followed by muffled shouting through the gag as his predicament came into view. He was cuffed, arms tied, but managed to squirm violently. As he did so, the ankle chains I'd fitted made a jangling like the ringing of a distant church bell. The night had taken on a purplish, blood-like quality as it overwhelmed the evening, curling around the inside of the van like some ancient spirit urging us on to a forsaken end. Kobi and I both wore balaclavas and would occasionally glance at each other with a murderous hardness I had preferred to think afflicted only him but now seeped between us like those memories that forge an unbreakable friendship.

We continued north, avoiding main roads. Some miles outside London, Kobi turned down an almost-invisible country track, then, ten minutes in, pulled up to a concrete structure built originally, I guessed, to house farm equipment.

A healthier part of me always hoped for a cleaner outcome: a nice discussion with Barker, which saw him back off my childhood friend, maybe even promise to look out for him along the way. Now this healthier part had to tell itself that it was the hooligan's refusal to listen that had gotten him here; the stubborn stupidity of a man just too accustomed to having power on his side.

We picked up our wriggling bundle with some difficulty until Kobi smashed it in the stomach with the billy club, at which point he became dead weight. As we approached the door, I noticed I was sweating but not from the effort. Some deep internal being screamed to run now, to not cross the threshold into Kobi's lockup.

The drab box inside was lit by a single bare bulb and contained one tiny window above head height, which had been snuffed out with paint. The dirty floor was stained in places by the deep black of something that could have been congealed blood. A sturdy wooden table stood in the middle adorned with leather restraints. Kobi had once again been overtaken by the spirit of annihilation. There was nothing to say between us and I could barely look his way lest he decide Barker would not be enough tonight. We threw the small man onto the concrete floor. He spat out the dirty gag, vomited, then got up on his knees, twisting himself to look up like the cornered animal he really was. In that moment, I had to give it to him, he was still full of menace.

"Do you know what you've fucking gotten into, you clueless cunts? Do you realise who we are, who I am?"

There was only one question. That single thing

whose heaviness had steadily escalated since a first reply from the belligerent currency trader.

"Why didn't you listen to me? My instructions. Why not just come alone and do the deal? It would have been so easy."

The death-bringing reptile who'd been called Kobi stood quietly behind me, swaying gently back and forth, waiting for its time.

Wade Barker replied only with eyes from which burst a searing hatred. I stepped forward and stuck him on the jaw with my steel knuckle enhancer, which put him down. He quickly got back up on his haunches, shaking his head in disgust.

"You fucking cowards. You ain't even got the balls to show me your faces! You know why I didn't listen? Because we do what we want. We don't let anyone tell us what's gonna happen. Least of all Chris Mason and his firm of scared little girls. My boys know it's him already. Put him on the phone right now and let me describe to him myself how bad his life is about to get."

And there I finally saw what it was; that this had all been some disastrous misunderstanding. I almost laughed. The man was looking through the only lens he possessed. He had figured all along that he'd been dealing with a rival gang. And he still did.

Barker held out a strong forearm on which had been tattooed the cross of St George.

"See this? You know what it means? It means I have

the heart of a lion. Come on and do your worst. It's nothing compared to what will happen to you!"

Before I could try and stop him, Kobi removed his face covering and shook his head at the man. My body wretched anticipating horrors it couldn't yet imagine. Kobi's first words were spoken casually, an afterthought as he walked to a large, padlocked box in the corner where he kept some tools.

"Your phone's back in the tunnel. St George wasn't English. He never even set foot on British soil."

He turned from studying the implements that the box contained.

"Do your worst. That's what your mate Drysdale said – at the beginning anyway."

A thousand varieties of human suffering condensed into a single moment on Wade Barker's face. I stayed to watch the first act then, in delirium, moved to leave. The butcher turned his neck from the table and the dead glaze of eyes seemed to register some kind of acknowledgement before hungrily returning to what nourished them.

There was a small scrambler by the side of the building for a quick getaway across the fields, so I took the van, abandoning it many miles from my place before jogging home. It was way past midnight and all I could see was Wade Barker's straining face, slobbering mucus and spit as he cried in agony for his mother.

17

SUNDAY

The balcony saw several glasses of cognac go down to stop my shaking hands before the crash towards unconsciousness. It was risky to be at home, but there were passports, Frank Okello's little blue book and nowhere else to be. Acceptance of death was creeping over me, one resistant cell at a time. If Royal Africa's killers had my name and address, avoiding them would likely only prolong the suffering for a few hours.

Morning rushed forward promptly and was accompanied by a soreness of spirit and body. Bright light seared into my eyes and my back ached like it was forty years older. I packed a soft tan leather holdall and headed towards the train station, calling Ashley several times on the way and getting nothing. The gun had been secreted into a false cupboard installed by the side of my kitchenette. It would take trained men at least an hour to uncover.

Accepting death was beginning to have unanticipated benefits. I was less jumpy about wide-open spaces and the future in general. Then there was the urge to draw a line under unfinished sentences; to gain some sense of ending with the only person who might mourn my disappearance now Kate was gone.

Sunday morning visiting hours at the Maudsley were no different to any other. My mother was wheeled in, then swollen legs shuffled the final couple of metres to her chair. I looked about the brightly coloured room and constructed a smile for her, which was met with a combination of confusion and suspicion.

"I'm off to Ghana."

"Guyana?"

"No, Ghana, Mum. West Africa. Two countries down from Nigeria."

"Oh. They don't like each other, Ghanaians and Nigerians, do they?"

She flashed a cunning, brown-toothed smile.

"Think that was back in the day, Mum. Less of an issue now."

"Can't blame the Ghanaians though really, can ya? Nigerians are bloody liars to a man!"

"I am not sure I will be back, Mum."

She carried on the conversation with herself without any real need for me to be there at all.

"But then your Ghanaian's probably no different to your average Nigerian."

Her face soured angrily.

"Joseph. Africans are forsaken people. Always have been and always will be. It's there in the bible!"

I breathed heavily to maintain some sense of calm.

"Mum, that's generally referred to as racism nowadays."

She looked up, hurt that her only child wasn't agreeing with such an obvious point of view, couldn't even do so to soothe the demons that blighted her pointless life. A bubble of spit formed at the left corner of her mouth as she leaned in to whisper some last vital advice.

"You don't see it now, Joseph, but you'll find out one day. Life will get you if you let those Nigerians near it! That goes for Ghanaians too. Stay away from 'em Joseph, stay away!"

There was a place fashioned from early childhood, where I went to deal with this type of assault. I met her shining, puffy face with total blankness, as if my deletion was what she really craved. It still worked its magic, and as the hatred drained from her features, my mind returned to a more normal mode of operation.

"Listen, Mum. This may be the last time for us. I wanted to tell you that I forgive you for this, for everything you've become. I understand a bit more now… that we are made by what happens to us… to us as children… unless we somehow find a way to rewrite that program. I don't know what happened to the child you, Mum, but it must have been truly fucking terrible."

Her eyes darted about in their fleshy housings, anticipating the stealthy blows usually hidden in my words, which, for once, simply weren't there. The legs of my chair grated the floor as I rose then bent at the waist to kiss her greasy hair. When I pulled back, I could see a tear on her cheek and it felt somehow like a triumph because finally and for the first time, maybe, she'd heard my voice through the yelling inside her head.

I called Yiolanda from the waiting gate at Heathrow. Children played, weaving in and out of walls and columns that secretly held everything up above us like some witch's spell. Yiolanda picked up as her voicemail message started.

"Hello, Joseph?"

"Hey, Y. I'm off to Ghana in fifty minutes and wondering if you could send me your friends' details… in case I need them."

"Consider it done!"

"Thanks."

The awkwardness of our last meeting came into view, boldly reinserting itself into the present.

"Well, uh. Have a great time, J…"

"Yiolanda – how I was at your shop. I am not going crazy. I will explain some time. It's work and stuff."

"OK, sure. Safe flight. Let's talk when you get back."

It felt enough that she understood that I understood it needed explaining.

Then children were called back to their parents and held tightly and, like some jurassic era centipede, a procession undulated forward onto the plane. It was made of immigrants returning to a source from which they hoped to draw energy in as many ways as there were stories. In some adults, I read the tension of the upcoming flight. Or maybe it was born of returning to greet the ghosts of an unsatisfactory past life, of having to don an outfit that no longer really fit so well. But for others, there was the soaring expectation of escaping to the relief of a place where they could simply be themselves without fear of sanction, to enjoy the dividend that flows from being in the majority.

In that queue, waiting to get on the old 747, selected to fly Africans back to Africa, some of my burden unfurled, stretching itself out with a languid relief in the full glare of daytime. It was, I realised then, a load borne by a child caught in the race war that was supposed to be a marriage.

18

SUNDAY EVENING

I was woken by my father, who looked at me tenderly and bade me come with him. He held my hand gently down the greyish-purple hallway, and, entering the kitchen, I felt the comfort of his grip vanish. I crossed into the orange-tinged light of our living room and there she was, my mother, naked, sitting in the stench of her own faecal mess. The rolls of fat at her waist undulated gently to the silent music she was playing from a miniature golden flute. She looked at me and it was time. In an instant, she was up and sprinting towards the balcony door. I chased her frantically but only got to the edge in time to see her greying body crash, a piece of meat escaped from the abattoir, onto the pavement below.

I held onto the balcony as it started swaying and then woke up instantly as the ageing plane hit some turbulence somewhere over the Sahara Desert. I was seventeen when the final leg of my mother's disease hit. Those were bad days as she lay on the sofa, unable to move for the weight of what was on her. I took refuge at homes of friends and on street corners after school where there were a variety of ways to burnish talents that would be needed for the adult life that was calling.

A slightly stressed stewardess asked if I was OK and needed anything. The processed lunch offered by her airline, had been missed and she was really hoping I didn't want it now. I honoured her need to not do her job and focused for the rest of the bumpy flight on the little blue book Frank Okello had gifted me on Newington Green. Here the Royal African Holdings empire was unpacked with, obsessive precision. I annotated it at certain points and, in an empty back page, jotted the bones of a survival plan, which would start in Accra.

The plane's wheels came to a screaming halt. We were walked a sweet short distance through various layers of disinterested officialdom, then spat out into the ocean of waving hands and faces stood waiting for arrivals. In the middle of this unfamiliar sea, my lifeboat appeared, Gifty Quarshie, a beautiful woman in her late twenties, who seemed to glide more than walk towards me. She was smiling and pointing at the car park where her driver was waiting.

"So, Joseph Wright, you made it to Ghana. Lucky us!"

Gifty had been raised in a household where a man,

her father, had felt a strong need to have two women marry him rather than one. So, both wives and their children (Gifty was her mother's only child but wife number one had managed five) existed in a heightened state of intrigue and alert in a large, detached house located in a soon-to-be sought-after suburb of South London. Gifty's polygamous father had bought the place somehow for cash in the early 1980s, when people like Uncle Ernest were failing to persuade the banks to let them in on the property game. The beneficial impact of her father's financial acumen was more than cancelled in magnitude by the painful toll that living like this had on all involved in satisfying Quarshie Senior's burgeoning mother complex.

Gifty had adapted to the dysfunctional environment in which her early years were spent by treating everything as a joke, which meant almost every second sentence was created with her tongue set firmly in that sculpted high-boned cheek.

Hers was one of my first proper engagements. When the needy polygamist had died before his time, as so many West African men seem to do, the toxicity at home had gone nuclear: eight people under one roof fighting over money that could make or break their lives. Gifty had stopped eating there for fear of poisoning, and her mother seemed to experience some kind of mental breakdown.

The issue was that of the dead multi-husband's wishes for his estate. More specifically, there had been a will in which he expressed the desire to share his well-earned wealth in half between the two women. A month into the process, another will had suddenly appeared in which his wishes seemed to have changed to share the estate in line with the number of children each had given him. The new allocation was fairer in some ways, but it reduced Gifty and her mother's share from a half to a sixth, which, given the sums involved, was a significant amount.

While her mother stumbled, the twenty-year-old woman's true metal came to the fore. She spent only a day weighing the options then called me through a friend of a friend. We went for a walk on the Rye; I asked her some questions and chewed things over a bit. Nowadays I'd have been onto it quicker, but within twelve hours I had asked Frank Okello to pillage a solicitor's computer files. The man was serving as executor of the first will.

Twenty-four hours later, I was sitting in the small office of P. J. Essien LLB, waiting for the boss to take a piss. When he returned, I told him I knew what he was up to, possessed proof and would have him disbarred unless he stopped. The fifty-year-old Ghanaian lawyer had acquired a very strong Tory-English accent, perhaps a sales pitch, which had succeeded so well that it had stuck. He became agitated as he saw that this was having no effect on a young mongrel working-class boy who wasn't worthy to shine his lovely Oxford shoes.

Although cornered, he wasn't a big man, so I was

very much surprised when he jumped to attack me, which allowed him to land a blow of sorts to my head. I learnt that day that you never know how someone will react under stress until you see them under it. Within a few seconds, I had brutally shown the older man what years of hard fight training could do to him if he continued to run this particular scam.

As he lay deflated and pained on the floor, I suggested he could either cut his losses here by extracting a decent fee from the side who'd hired him to invent the new will or face total disgrace and more treatment of the sort I'd just given him.

Gifty and her mother got their half of the money and immediately moved themselves to Accra, away from the multitude of slights and aggressions of a day-to-day life in Britain.

"You married yet, G?"

She sung a loud laugh.

"I am waiting for the right person, Joseph. That perfect guy. He must be very well-off, old enough to be on his last legs and not at all interested in sex."

I liked Gifty, even if I didn't really know her. I felt the survivor in her.

"Like a benevolent uncle? Why, you spent all that money I got for you?"

"Now, now, Jo!" she said, eyes wide and staring at the back of her silent driver. "You know Mummy went and spent almost all of it on the house. We barely have enough to pay Kwabena here."

"Yeah. I hear that houses are expensive as hell in Accra. Must be hard to make ends meet."

Gifty nodded in slow appreciation at my facility for lying. Outside, I stretched the depression from my limbs and took in the sweet tang of an Accra evening, which truly felt like music for a soul that had lost connection to the many joys of simply existing. But arriving in Ghana had already lowered my guard, making a home for stupidity where astuteness should have sat watch. And carrying on that way would see me gone as quickly as a wounded deer in a river of alligators.

"You sure you don't want to come home, Joseph? We have plenty of space."

"No... I... I don't want to get you in any trouble."

"Trouble? You've really gotten my interest now! I have a reliable man for you; his name's Michael and he drives my aunt when she's here. We've also got a Land Cruiser as requested, sir!" She gave a fake salute. I felt desire nudge quietly against the faint possibility of a different life.

"The car will be about two hundred pounds a day, I think."

"OK, thanks. I'll be needing Michael at 5am tomorrow if possible. Before the famous Accra traffic gets going."

"Phew, you are serious! And where are you off to?"

"Better you don't know, G. Really."

Comfort's Lodge, the brown stucco-finished guest house in which Gifty had me staying, was presided over by a group of sisters. I never found out how many, but all had inherited strong genes from the same person across time.

This evening, the front desk was staffed by two of the brood, who both gave me a similar look of curious efficiency as they took details and a sterling deposit upfront.

"Which one of you is Comfort?" I asked, attempting to reinvent myself into the charming tourist for the week.

"That was our mother," the older sibling stated sadly.

"Was?"

"She passed less than a year after building this for us."

"Sounds like she was a serious woman."

"She was a nurse in Britain but brought us back to finish secondary school here while she got the money over there to fund the hotel. She worked two jobs for twenty years so that we could have this in Ghana."

The younger sister glanced up, wanting to get a word in, but some unwritten pecking order took her eyes down again and kept her lips closed.

"I can see her in both of you," I gambled. "That must be some solace having lost her so early."

Smiling eyes told me I'd made friends with the guess.

"How did I know that?" I said, grinning back, noticing how free I felt here even with the threat of death hovering overhead.

Older 'Comfort Junior' happily showed me to a room on the second floor. I lay down on the utilitarian bed still smiling, now at the whirring fan, then wondering why I felt this way. I didn't crave alcohol, wasn't hungry and was unperturbed by the cockroach that sprinted under a chipped brown chest of drawers. Sleep came quickly and it wasn't yet 10pm.

19

MONDAY MORNING

Mr Kwame Opoku-Brown, Deputy Director of the planning department of Ghana's Land Commission, didn't live in the crumbling quarters built for civil servants a lifetime ago, on the optimism of a newly born country. Opoku-Brown had, however, managed to build a significant homestead in a well-off suburb to the north of Accra's university campus. It was only ten minutes' drive for us against already-accumulating traffic going into town.

We parked a hundred metres away, which felt like a good time to break the ice with the steely man who'd picked me up bang on 5am, before the sun had even begun to offer its blessings on the day.

"Michael. Let me guess what you did before this."

The man was unaccustomed to laughing to order for his clients but obliged me with a nod in the rear-view mirror.

"You are fortyish, still very fit in a country where men with a decent job tend not to be by your age."

He forced a chortle at the back-handed compliment.

"Forty-six actually. Yes, Mr Wright – too much carbohydrate with their stew."

"You are punctual – not early, not late. You know how to be on time."

He continued to nod, enjoying my detective routine.

"Your shoes are well polished, shirt starched, trousers precisely ironed."

I left him hanging a while…

"Let me see… Army?"

He answered with a knowing smile in the mirror.

"Sergeant? Lesser ranks might well lose some of the habits a few years after they leave."

He nodded again and I'd finally drawn him in.

"Staff sergeant. You too, Mr Wright?"

"No. But I have been in a few battles. Understand why the discipline is needed. It is just for survival."

He turned his head to look at me straight this time as if I had answered a question that he hadn't quite asked himself yet.

"You know I did think about it when I was sixteen. Had I gone into the British Army, I would have made corporal at best and you would have been my boss's boss."

Michael shot an even harder glance, which spoke of a reflection on life's injustices.

"Why you leave the army? Money? You have kids to feed?"

"Oh I just got – I don't know. OK, yes. But Ghana doesn't offer many opportunities if you don't know the right people. You know what I mean?"

"Sure do, brother!"

"And I can make good money driving tourists or part-time Ghanaians around. They give great tips."

"Nice plant there, Michael!" I shouted laughing.

He offered a second understated grin.

At 6am on the dot, Opoku-Brown's new Japanese-made car jagged out of his compound and the entrepreneur masquerading as a bureaucrat drove to the office in a manner that did not fit his pay cheque. We followed him to the Land Commission buildings south of the airport, a journey of only a few miles, which took ninety minutes in the futility of the morning's crawling exhaust fumes. I rang Gifty as we parked.

"Hi, Joseph," Gifty sang, ever-willing to hear the voice of the man who had enabled her life to really begin.

"Tell me something. I am guessing Ghana is quite a small social scene for young people with money."

"I'm not so involved in it but sometimes it can be fun."

"John Toks Owusu. Half Nigerian, half Ghanaian, father a diplomat, posh accent, boarding school educated in England." As I spoke, I texted her the picture from the photo frame in Flo Danjuma's home, then the mobile number Frank had somehow obtained.

"Am I one of your detectives too now, Joseph? How much are you going to pay me?"

It was a good question the more I thought about it. Gifty had proven herself adept at survival, and here I was in Accra with nobody but her between the slim hope of life and likely death back in Britain.

"Let me think about that one, G. Can we get to Mr Owusu?"

"Wow, you took me seriously, you strange man! I'll find out where he goes and when. There's only a few places in Accra."

We ate breakfast near the Land Commission. Sitting out in the fresh morning sun, I was beginning to feel the former soldier could be more use than just driving me around.

"Michael. What happens to corrupt civil servants in Ghana?"

He clammed up just a little, which spoke its own tongue.

"If they are exposed in the press?"

"I wouldn't go that route with this man. Find another path. A thing that is as ubiquitous as the air we breathe isn't very newsworthy."

Two hours later, I walked into the faded bungalows of the Land Commission, which were slowly being claimed by the very red earth they purported to control. I was carrying a large presentation box of fine cognac in my leather bag, acquired in Heathrow's duty-free shops for personal use but now called to a higher purpose.

The receptionist looked me up and down.

"Yes?" he said, bored already.

"Hello. My company runs a prize for the African civil servant of the year."

"Which company?" He had perked up a touch and was actually listening now.

"Sandton Associates. Headquartered in Jo'burg. We have established a shortlist this year and, umm…"

I paused and pulled out Okello's blue book to check the name for effect.

"Deputy Director Opoku, Opoku…"

"Opoku-Brown?"

"That's it. He will be invited to our October ceremony in South Africa, all expenses paid, of course, to collect an award for a career of committed service to Ghana's people. My boss told me I am to deliver this invitation bottle to him in person and to confirm the travel details."

And so it went through a couple of long dark corridors, another gatekeeper and then the 'civil servant of the year's' meek personal assistant, for whom messing up her boss's chance at an award might have meant unemployment.

She'd given him the good news by the time I'd walked down to his bare office and the heavy, thick-necked functionary offered me a magnanimous smile befitting of a bureaucrat of award-winning standing. A large photograph of Ghana's president seemed to smile ironically as Brown gestured.

"Sit down, sit down, Mr?"

"Joseph Cosby, Deputy Director Opoku-Brown. It is an honour to meet you!" I shook his outstretched hand, gave him the business card I'd had made up after breakfast and offered the box of cognac with both hands.

"Something we give to all our award winners, sir."

He looked quietly pleased but maintained the demeanour of someone worthy of such an honour.

"Tell me about your organisation, Mr Cosby."

"Yes. We are deliberately very low key. We were set up on the wishes of a successful South African technology entrepreneur, Jacob Ndlovu. Mr Ndlovu's grand vision was to locate the best civil service careerists in Africa and, when they were close enough to retirement, to approach them to take up lucrative board and oversight roles across the continent. Think of it like a club of wisdom membered by people who might pass this on after their careers of national service are at an end. As an organisation, we operate purely on a non-profit basis for the good of Africa."

Opoku-Brown's irises doubled in width as the arrows of my fiction hit their intended targets. I wondered if some part of him saw the humour in it too as his hands began to rub tightly together in slow anticipation.

"I see! May I ask – how did you find me?"

"Ah! We spend many, many months researching and

refining our candidate database, Mr Opoku-Brown. We take into account length of service, effectiveness, commitment and, of course, treatment of junior colleagues."

He nodded with me.

"Of course. Passing on the torch has always been one of my touchstones."

I removed the file from the bag in which I had brought the cognac, opening it at a particular page.

"We naturally closely interrogate any work the candidates might have done more recently."

I slid the document across his empty desk. The glass louvres on the small mosquito-netted windows seemed to wink twice as Opoku-Brown shot me a lightning glance. He knew why I was here. There wasn't going to be a Johannesburg gala awards dinner, but I still looked like an asset from which might be extracted a healthy return. His shoulders relaxed a centimetre into the more familiar terrain of immediate personal enrichment.

"We would like to understand a bit more about what happened to this piece of land. Its ownership seems to have recently been reassigned somehow."

He met my glance fully and without mercy. I was playing in his backyard now and he wanted me to know it.

"The information you give me is confidential and valuable." His eyes remained fixed on me with an intensity of the predator evaluating how best to attack then consume its victim.

"How valuable?"

"Oh, let's say two hundred dollars for a ten-minute tutorial. Title: 'Facilitating Ways of Doing Business in Ghana'."

The crooked civil servant sniffed then shifted a big-stomached waist back into the comfort of the synthetic-padded boss's chair he'd called home for two decades. I eventually realised this was simply waiting for me to produce the cash. I slid my hand into the papers of the file and then opened at a page revealing two crisp hundred-dollar notes.

He held them up for inspection in the light – the forger's nemesis. I was on the clock now and so shot him a questioning stare.

"Because of the proximity of its colonial history, Ghana has a complex system of land tenure whereby traditional rights of chieftaincy coexist with more recent claims conferred by pre- and post-independence political regimes." The man sounded like he'd given the start of this lecture many times.

"So, I imagine this complexity gives rise to opportunities from time to time for ownership to be 'reassigned'."

Brown ignored my question. He wasn't going to give up the prize so easily.

"Most land is leased in Ghana, and leases typically last fifty years."

"OK. So rights to use valuable pieces of land, for example, acquired soon after independence, have been coming up for renewal in the last few years, I imagine. Do the leaseholders usually have automatic rights of renewal?"

"In theory, 'yes'… but then…" He became enlivened by the object that was the source of his money fountain.

"There is some area of grey in there and… and that's where we can offer help."

"I see. So purely hypothetically, a colonial-era operator of a valuable mine might one day wake up to realise they no longer had the ultimate right to operate it?"

"Yes, that is possible – hypothetically, of course."

"What recourse to law might they have?"

His answers fired back with a swiftness that made me wonder what good he might have done for his country in some parallel universe.

"That depends on a number of things. The first is how public they wanted to go about it. We do have due process of a sort here but… the courts are painfully slow and outcomes uncertain. It might take years to find out who ended up with the lease for their land, especially if most of the paper trail had somehow vanished. More importantly, though, it would expose someone who, let's say, had gained their rights 'incognito', to the possibility of public glare, even if they had powerful allies. Finally, it also depends who you are going up against. As a South African, I am sure you must understand the historical sensitivity of returning to us land that has been obtained under… shall we say… stressed colonising conditions."

I was surprised he had still bought the South African bit of my story but it hardly mattered. The man was in full flow and the last thing I needed was for it to stop. Gone was the sluggish bureaucrat who had accepted some imaginary award. In his place, the most astute of advisers who understood every trick in the book and had probably invented some more of his own for fun.

"So you'd have to be African to pull off this reassignment?"

"West African. You, for example, wouldn't have much of a chance."

"What about the chiefs in the area in question?"

"Again, that would depend on who they are, how scared they are or not and…"

"Their price?"

The predator nodded, enjoying exposing the full range of his hidden skillset without fear of reprisal.

"The land in the document contains an operating mine?"

His yellowing eyes calculated again – *how much for how much*? I put another two hundred inside the file. Things thickened between us. A fat fly that had been sitting on the desk started careering around in a demented motion banging against the window for escape.

"Many remote areas, Mr Cosby, are highly prospective from the viewpoint of mining and have maintained small artisanal operators for centuries."

"So there's lots of gold in them there hills but…"

His statement wasn't yet worth the bonus paid. He coughed with the formality of officialdom to make the key pronouncement.

"The presence of a large-scale gold-mining operation somewhere in this locality has not been recorded or catalogued anywhere or by anyone."

My mind whirred faster, breaths shortening.

"How would they manage to do that for fifty years?" But if anyone could, it would be them. I picked myself up again just in time to come back to draw one more sip from the corrupted well.

"How many of these types of hypothetical situations could exist out there in a country like Ghana? It must become increasingly risky the more that there are…"

"I don't know, Mr Cosby. More than you'd think probably because it might be very profitable." Opoku-Brown laid himself back in the loving embrace of his chair, quickly reassuming the persona of a bureaucratic koala. My lesson was over.

I got up to leave but then leaned in to take back the cognac.

"I am a violent person, Brown. It's my job, in fact. I was outside your lovely house this morning in North Legon. If I should meet any unexpected action while in your country, I will know where to come. If I am incapacitated, I have colleagues who will know where to come."

He didn't look at me this time, so I grabbed his

thick throat with one hand and forced his head up to meet my gaze so that he understood that I meant what I said.

I strolled out of the office slowly, digesting the conversation, down the decaying corridors through which I had gained false entry. Opoku-Brown had already been involved in scamming one of the powerful institutions in history so who knew if my final words would have any effect at all. But it didn't matter. I would probably be dead before I found out.

20

MONDAY NIGHT

"**M**ichael, how long will it take for us to get here?" I was pointing to a copy of the map I'd photographed from both Flo Danjuma's safe and Pastor Daniels' files. It was the one I'd shown Opoku-Brown a few minutes earlier.

He frowned.

"It's quite remote. That last few miles will be slow."

"We will have to do some on foot. I don't want them to know we are there. There's a thousand dollars in it for you."

Within an hour, we'd collected gear and were driving out of the city. I had changed to dark combat trousers, cross trainers and a black long-sleeved cotton T-shirt, packed for night-time activity. In a pocket sat a rectangular knuckle enhancer that appeared as innocuous under customs X-ray machines as a large tie clip. I called my guardian angel, who answered in the vaguely mocking style reserved for those she really liked.

"Detective Wright."

"G. I am up going up country with Michael. Back tomorrow."

"You are on a mission here."

"Yep. Could say that."

If she hadn't guessed the urgency of my visit to Ghana before, it was now dawning, and a note of concern entered the chords of her voice.

"Where are you going, Joseph?"

"Can't tell you but, umm… west… and north a bit. Michael will take care of me. You know he is a soldier."

"Well…" She didn't sound convinced.

I changed the topic partly because this woman may have had gravity to stop me, to fool myself that I didn't have to go anywhere, that I could stay in Ghana and enjoy the life I really deserved.

"How's our friend John Owusu doing?"

"He likes to go to a bar called Ruby off Liberation Road."

"Well, maybe we could catch up with him tomorrow evening before I get the late plane – that road's near the airport, right?"

"You leaving tomorrow, Joseph? You've only been here a minute!"

"Argh – it's a long story, Gifty. One day. One day when I've gotten past this thing. Hopefully."

The lonely wear in my voice was enough for her to stop and for Michael to flex some tension out of his shoulders as he drove.

"OK, OK. See you tomorrow. Good luck, JJ, with whatever it is."

We took the Cape Coast Road at high speed, the wash of the Atlantic to our left and a fertile yet somehow barren landscape to our right, which rushed north for three hundred miles towards evisceration in the embrace of the desert. Then, after a few hours, we turned north too, away from the freshness of fine sea spray into lush tropical hillsides, across small towns and villages where people eked out lives, loved and died as anonymously as anyone else on the planet. As the satellite navigation system faded into the countryside, the roads narrowed, the foliage about them thickened, then they quickly became tracks of compacted clay, trails leading to unknown places. A few miles from our destination, Michael swerved sharply to avoid what looked like a large pile of old clothes on the road and broke dead before we smashed into the earth bank that bordered the dirt track.

"Was it a rock?"

Michael turned with heaviness in his eyes.

"A person. Probably someone ejected from their community with nowhere to go."

Images of my mother's sofa-ridden dejection resurfaced.

"Mental illness. A suicide attempt. Lie in the road and hope someone hits you."

"You could call it that. I don't know. I don't speak the dialect here, but we could try go back and see."

"No. It'll be dark in two hours."

Twenty minutes later, Michael pulled up.

"This is as good as we will get. There's a hill to climb two miles to the east. Something's there."

"How do you know?"

"We are in the middle of the bush, but there is still some type of decent road. It must go somewhere for a reason."

By the time we arrived at the summit, the evening cicadas had commenced their percussive warnings. We crouched quickly as the camp came into view below. Michael let out a muffled cry.

"Oh God!"

A person had been strung up high on a pole in the middle of a set of ageing prefabricated structures. He had died hanging there after a number of days and flies were now gathering, eagerly drawn by sweet decay they could sense just under the skin.

To the north and east of the compound, as we looked down and beyond the buildings, a large tunnel had been dug directly into the side of the hill opposite. At 5:20pm, a horn sounded and groups of dazed men started to emerge into the dying light, all so thin that it seemed impossible they could have done anything more down there than toil to keep breathing.

The compound had no fences but we counted a dozen blue-uniformed guards strolling healthily around the zombie-like captives, rapping the odd back or arm from time to time or shouting at people too exhausted to be terrified.

The wails of cicadas grew louder as I retrieved a small camera from the pocket of my trousers. The steely presence of Michael had hardened into an even tougher metal. There was no need to say what tormented him. I understood because I felt it too through some inherited channel: the suffering of millennia of enslaved humanity.

"First, I get some evidence," showing him the tiny electronic miracle. "It's going to be dark soon."

"Then we go in with a plan." The staff sergeant wasn't asking.

Before night came, the slaves were lined up to receive their meagre daily portions at a wooden table ten metres from the cadaver on the pole. They sat outside on the clay-red earth eating intently from metal bowls with unwashed hands.

At 6:16pm, a whistle blew enthusiastically and the greying ends of men staggered to bare feet. In all, nearly two hundred souls were counted off one by one into three wooden barns. Thick metal bars were then wedged into the door handles to prevent escape.

The night's stars shone hopefully in a pure-black sky over the screaming of a million invisible insects. The points of light were so clear it was as if we'd been taken up past the atmosphere into the vacuum of space. The long sheds where the enslaved were imprisoned found themselves pincered on three sides by a further six prefabricated structures housing staff and equipment. One smaller building, sitting at the entrance to the horseshoe, served as some kind of common room where guards would arrive and leave with bottles in hand.

Once past the outskirts to the clearing, we split up. I headed for the smaller brightly lit building, the humanity in my eyes deadening under the muslin of violence. Crouching low, I darted my head up to side-window height. A muscular, red-headed guard and his lean African colleague were lounging in rattan armchairs watching a Nollywood soap while getting drunk on beer.

From the room beyond this, a shortish girl, maybe fifteen years old, entered, quietly followed by an older, bald custodian, who was doing his belt up theatrically. The two seated men looked at each other as if deciding by some telepathic device whose turn was next. The girl drank some water from the sink of the room's corner kitchen, then stood pensively, head bowed, bracing for the next rapist to step up. The belt-doer said something on his way out of the door and all three laughed loudly.

I waited for the red head to grab the girl's upper arm, yanking her towards the bedroom, leaving the lean guard alone to watch various Nigerian intrigues unfold on the small screen. It took me only a few seconds to open the door and be on him, shifting my weight so fully into the blow, as he turned to look at me, that I felt the metal knuckle enhancer break bone and push the material constituting his nose into his face towards the brain.

I moved swiftly, opening the door to see the guard's buttocks rising and falling upon the girl. He had been quick, not even bothered to take his trousers fully off. She saw me first. Her eyes pleaded for help as I raised the truncheon taken from the common room and brought it crashing onto the back of the grunting man's skull. The red head arched his spine in seizure before falling face down, dead weight on top of her. She caught my eyes again but didn't scream – she'd experienced worse. I pulled her out, then we sat for a while adjusting to realities of which neither had dared to dream only a few minutes before. I flexed my neck, then straightened up and gestured for her to get dressed and come with me.

Outside, yelling had started from three of the units that housed the guards. Michael had jammed the doors before setting them alight with petrol we'd obtained from the site's truck. The painful death he offered was neither emotional nor vindictive, merely a solution to the problem of their superior numbers. We met at the vehicle, barely acknowledging each other before stalking off to inflict liberation and hurt in equal measure. Yells of the guards ghosted into screams as the skeleton-like workers teetered around the compound, tasting distant freedom through the smoke and stench of petrol-burnt flesh. I pointed them all to the truck as I found them. A few went as instructed, but others merely wandered off as if asleep at the wheel of their one opportunity to stay alive.

A couple of the guards had managed to break through a window, and as they crawled on the earth gasping for air, I clubbed them brutally about the head until they stopped moving.

Michael had located the site's equipment store and was setting off calamitous explosions of dynamite at regular intervals from the entrance to the mine. In the flickering dark, I felt more than saw a blow coming from over my right shoulder, ducking left, away and under the glint of dulled metal, then swivelling to see the yelling attacker fall onto his face with the force he'd just used trying to kill me. I didn't let him get up, jumping onto the rising body, hitting terror-gripped arms with the truncheon before he could grasp his cutlass. I breathed steadily to keep landing then little by little, his defences gave in. Soon the body relaxed to the floor and his pleading eyes held no sign at all.

I sprinted back to the truck and counted about twenty people in the back, including the girl. They looked up from sunken eyes unable to fully comprehend what was unfolding, just a bunch of stinking rags, taking meagre comfort from the closeness of the huddle. I double-backed, picking up a few more of the zombies on the way. When I returned to the truck a third time, Michael was seated and ready to go. We didn't speak; we neither smiled in triumph nor cried with despair. He had surprised me, but, somehow, I hadn't him. He'd simply known who I was from the moment we'd met.

Michael followed the road until it came to our Land Cruiser, then we drove the two vehicles in convoy for a couple of hours, depositing our cargo of people outside a hospital run by nuns, in a small town that Michael knew well. The truck was wiped clean and abandoned at a breaking yard, which was unlikely to ask questions of a gift horse such as this. It wasn't yet 2am when Michael dropped me outside Comfort's Lodge. We nodded, under the grim kinship that shared violence can impart.

"See you at 11am tomorrow."

The soldier registered my words, turned the Jeep around, then sped off into the void of Accra city.

21

TUESDAY

As they re-formed into wakefulness, the images seemed born of a difficult dream state: emaciated bodies of slaved miners, a human carcass impaled on its pole. But the look on the girl's face when I rolled the weight of the guard off her naked body brought me quickly to the cold order of things. I showered, rang Gifty and left a message.

The next one went to a British mobile phone.

"Mr Folarin."

"Joseph? I didn't recognise the number."

"I've changed phones."

My client hadn't known the dangerous path he'd set me down, but some piece of me felt him at fault. I wanted to pass on instructions that might help save him but also ached to donate some of the bitter fear I had tasted the over the last few days.

"I'm ringing to tell you what's next."

He was confused and it wasn't time for that.

"Asante is dead, as is the lawyer Lawrence Michaels."

The second part shook him up. It was one thing for a nobody immigrant to be taken, but a white lawyer working for a leading City firm?

"Dead? Both of them? But this is the United Kingdom, not some lawless narco-state?"

"Maybe the people we are dealing with fly above the rest, Mr Folarin. I don't know and telling you more won't help you. My life is under threat and it's time you move as far away from me as you can. Get a new phone, email address. Change your name if possible and also where you stay. I would consider returning to Nigeria too. It might be safer there."

A third sister was sitting at the hotel's reception when I checked out, this one aged about forty.

"Leaving early? I hope everything was to your liking."

"Yes, it was good."

She relaxed a touch.

"You know, I wish I'd had a parent like your mother. Someone prepared to donate their very life into strong foundations built for their children's future."

She was surprised but not greatly. The statement sounded as true as maternal promises.

Michael was waiting in the newly washed Jeep, heavy in spirit. The previous night's tragedies had cost him too.

"Let's go see our friend at the Land Commission."

I handed him the thousand dollars owed; we shook hands, locking eyes for a painful slice of time.

Opoku-Brown was engaged in a double-portioned lunch at a nearby outdoor soup joint when I got to him. He spotted me too late to escape and a dozen calculations passed behind the still yellowing eyes, which fixed me with silent menace. I ignored their intentions and didn't stand on ceremony.

"Wanted to show you this film I made. It's a slave compound somewhere you might know."

He winced at the impaled corpse onto which I had focused and zoomed. After a minute watching, the bureaucrat looked up.

"Were they Ghanaians?"

"No. Guards neither. They were acquired from all over Africa but does that matter?"

His shrug suggested it did.

"Guess the pan-African dream dies here."

To my surprise, the cornered man started eating again, maybe out of a compulsion to soothe his fear, to buy time, or it could have been that he'd simply learnt not to waste a good meal.

He finished quickly and dipped the hands he'd used to feed himself in a small bowl containing a thoughtfully placed slice of lemon to break up the grease.

"What do you want, Mr Cosby?"

I managed a sad smile.

"What does any young person want from the generation that preceded them?"

Turning the film on again, I could see from the stress lines of his moon-like face that my tone was transmitting more menace. He was uncomfortable, adrift from the familiar set of scripts life had shown him how to perform.

"Some integrity? Diligence? A bit of wisdom? And how about some self-love?"

Brown backed away in the plastic chair, wary of the damage I might do before anyone got there to stop it.

"Who first approached you to take the land title? Let me see: John Owusu? How about Lawrence Michaels or perhaps… Yaw Asante?" There's something about known facts that most people find hard not to register somewhere on their faces or in an involuntary movement unless, like Kobi, they are constituted at the core by an absence of feeling. Opoku-Brown shifted slightly to his left as he heard the last name but he knew all three.

"Yaw Asante then, the former police chief. Guess he still had some old contacts here that got him to you."

The deputy director didn't like being read so easily and his jaw set in obdurate resistance.

"It's time you understood some things. Asante has disappeared. He was led away from his London flat by three mercenaries in a green Mercedes. He was so scared he went voluntarily. Probably under torture, he gave up Lawrence Michaels, who has also vanished. Now their affairs and online footprint are being slowly run down by someone. As far as I can see, there's only one person left for their killers to chase – the fool who signed the paperwork."

"And where is that paperwork, Mr Cosby?" The predator reappeared, briefly emboldened by the safety of his document shredder.

"You imagine you've covered your tracks, but I found copies of the land forms twice in four days. How do you think I got to you? If Asante gave up Michaels, what's the betting they asked him about you too? These people will be coming. Watch this film and see what they really think of us. We mean nothing to them. You'll be just another one of millions dead at their hand."

The truth of my words landed hard. Opoku-Brown belched in panic and sweat started to gash down his forehead into his eyes. You could almost feel sorry for him. I snapped the horror film off the table and stood so sharply that his palms had only come up for protection once I was turning to walk away.

Michael drove us to the bit of the ocean upon which Accra unsteadily balances. I mostly stumbled past retail traps and restaurant staff paid to harass unfamiliar passers-by. Then onto a beach, once the pride of a city but now as far from that word as it was possible to travel.

A lone horse trotted up, stopped briefly to engage, jutting ribcage straining against thinning hide, then moved tiredly on. The grey sea had dragged what seemed like a million pieces of strewn plastic reluctantly out into itself and then vomited as many as it could back onto the sand with the backwash. I cleared a patch and sat down, hugging my knees, wanting to be soothed by that crashing of the ocean, as fundamental somehow as the pulse of a mother's heart to a foetal soul.

Michael crouched next to me on his toes. I turned to him, quiet tears staining my cheeks.

"It is how we lose, Michael. How we have lost. It's been centuries. What's wrong with us, with this place?"

He placed a gentle hand on my shoulder.

"It's just like other places. Some good and some bad things. That's all."

I rested my head on his shoulder. He shifted himself to get closer, then put a strong arm around me. And then I wept quietly with the sorrow of a child dragged away to the orphanage. He stayed like that for as long as it took, an act of unconditional tenderness beyond any I had known before.

22

TUESDAY

"**W**oah, what's happened to you?"

Gifty was all sisterly concern.

"What do you mean?"

"You look knackered or ill or something!"

I checked myself in a mirror of the well-stocked bar, which wouldn't have been out of place in a Mayfair restaurant. I could see what she meant. There were darker areas of rough under my eyes, hair jutted out at unkempt angles, and my skin seemed to have acquired a greenish tinge to it.

"It's been a tough week, Gifty. I…"

"Ah, here he is!" she piped enthusiastically as a young well-dressed man in his late twenties rolled in with a friend. The men were laughing whilst jostling for top position in the eligible bachelor of the year competition. Gifty wasted no time approaching them.

"Hi. Toks, right?"

The men fashioned their best male-model smiles. Gifty was beautiful and breathed the same slightly strange air that bridges West Africa and Britain.

"Hi. And you are…" Toks's accent matched his London business partner's almost perfectly.

"Gifty. We met once at a party. I was with my friend Akosua Mills."

The men nodded as if subjected to the power of some master hypnotist.

"I am here with my half-brother Joseph, having a few drinks before he takes the plane back to London. He hates flying, you know – look what it's done to him!"

'Half-brother' was really clever. She was still inviting them in and had neutralised me as a competitor.

We soon ended up at a table eating sliders and drinking cognac. The bar was decorated in a chic art deco style, surrounded on three sides by huge glass windows looking down onto the major Accra artery of Liberation Road, but far enough away that we couldn't see the young children begging at traffic lights.

Toks and his friend concentrated mostly on Gifty and on me only in relation to how it placed her.

"So, Joseph, what do you do back in London?"

"I am a risk consultant." The well-manicured eyebrows rose, both impressed and a touch sceptical at the same time.

"I see. Which firm?"

"I work for myself, Toks. Clients only come to me if they have very serious issues that need solving. Not one case is the same. That's what keeps me interested in it."

The Ghanaian's scepticism graduated rapidly to disbelief. With top-level contacts, it was just about possible in Nigeria maybe, but a twenty-something black guy in Britain? His left hand reached to the gold cufflink of his right wrist, fiddling out the agitation of having to tolerate yet another boring fantasist.

"I'll give you an example. You know Everett Langston?"

"Yeah, heard the name. He's one of Britain's most successful black businessmen. Always hard to tell how successful though as he keeps himself to himself."

"I've done stuff for him across the operation. I work off referrals only."

"That's impressive. Pretty feast and famine, I imagine."

I laughed.

"Yeah definitely. But when it rains, let me tell you, it really does pour!"

The men tossed glances at each other, assigning to me some kind of invisible grade. I ordered the next round of drinks to make sure I had passed, then we moved on to the usual cocktail of conversation that formed the social oxygen for Africa's young elites: gossip about politicians' children that they knew, stories of billionaire Nigerian businessmen, nightclubs and wild parties. As they did so, my mind drifted towards the staff sergeant who was sat in the car below still playing driver.

Gifty easily covered for my awkwardness. I kept a check on the amount I was drinking as the two men became louder with the hand that alcohol usually deals. People stopped to pay homage, hoping some of what was here would rub off. Others merely shook hands and sprinted to the safety of less successful tables.

Gifty excused herself to the bathroom and the two Ghanaians were suddenly left without a purpose. But she'd picked the perfect moment to carry me to this point. The woman was that good.

"So, Toks, I've told you about me, so let me guess what your game is?"

He flashed a perfect-toothed grin.

"Bet I can guess it near enough."

"You wanna bet real money, Joseph, my maybe-new friend?"

"How about those cufflinks – they're stunning?"

"Oh no, not for gambling, fella. These are an Adinkra symbol of our ancestors made from Ghana's purest gold. *Bese Saka*! They bring me good luck."

"What does it mean?"

Owusu leaned in for dramatic effect, cognac laced heavily into every breath.

"It symbolises the essence of the cola nut. Abundance, affluence, true wealth in unity!"

The drunk men giggled childishly at Owusu's performance.

"I definitely wouldn't be betting that kind of luck away. How about a hundred dollars then? Should buy a round or two here at least."

Another exchange of quick glances suggested the outsider was pushing his boundaries.

"OK, Joseph. Let's see what you got."

"You went to boarding school in Britain so are very well-connected here in Ghana because you come from money. You did well enough at school to enter one of the UK's so-called professions. I'm thinking finance. Not the gambling bit, the technical side; corporate advisory maybe? You came back to Ghana to use your connections as you quickly realised it was a way more attractive life than being a failing black cog in the white corporate machine."

"He's good!" The two laughed more nervously than before.

"You are on the up. Out on a Tuesday living large and everyone knows you here. You must work for yourself like I do because there's no arsehole of a boss to indulge in the morning."

"I've got my hundred dollars ready, Joseph. Please stop before you reveal the colour of my underpants – you win!"

I smiled, the gracious victor, and we all chuckled some more.

"How about we put that hundred into the pot for the round of drinks next time we meet?"

"How about you tell us more about risk, Jo – you don't mind if I call you that?"

"Ah, risk. Maybe this example nails it down a bit more. I've got a client I can't name who owns a valuable portfolio of assets. Can't tell you where because they prize my discretion above all else."

The men were still smiling indulgently.

"But I can tell you they are gold mines. My client's issue is how to stop some local, let's say… 'people of influence' adjusting the paperwork to undermine their ownership of these mines." John Owusu's grin disappeared as fast as a bullet to the head. His left hand returned to the comforter of the gold cufflink and a twitch in the temple sang its own ballad of truth.

"I keep telling them the only way to address risk in this case is to share ownership carefully with the right partners. They don't want to do this, as it looks like weakness. You know these white people have been in charge for so long, they still think the world revolves around their unlimited capacity for violence."

The table slumped into the kind of thoughtful pause that happens at a funeral. It was time to leave. I got up to shake hands, and on cue, Gifty appeared to exchange pleasantries, numbers and chaperone me to the airport.

Outside, the humidity felt like it could draw every toxin from a body willing to stay in its presence for long enough. Michael zoomed up precisely with the oversized jeep for the short journey to the airport.

It was tough to say goodbye to Gifty, casting down the diamonds of my fleeting dreams in favour of the worthless stones that life would now throw at me back in Britain. But to Gifty's surprise, it was even harder to say goodbye to Michael, who I clutched tightly, whispering repeatedly the words. "Thank you, Uncle, thank you!"

23

WEDNESDAY

I noticed the feeling that I was being followed sometime after leaving Yaw Asante's flat at about 2pm. There was no moment of revelation, just a creeping discomfort that pricked away until I was forced to pay attention to it. Maybe it was just tiredness. The bumpy six-hour flight and early landing offered insufficient rest for even the most committed sleeper. Then there was also the effect of what I had just found in Yaw Asante's Hackney home. Once the feeling was set though, I knew I had only one last piece to bring onto the board, and he was almost as likely to extinguish my life as those following me. I had called Kobi, my best friend, who I now knew had a lockup somewhere past North London where he committed crimes against humanity for pleasure.

Far earlier, when the day was barely opening, Frank Okello, the Ugandan IT genius, had been the first name I'd messaged, jostling with hundreds of sleepy passengers towards the unforgiving stare of the UK's border officers. Those in charge of landing slots had decided to have the flight from Lagos put down at a similar time, perhaps to get the whole West African issue out of the way first. We agreed to meet at a coded location after which my phone found the nearest airport bin and I headed for the train to Central London.

I met Frank down by Regents Canal where the old piece of man-made river passes under the bowels of London Zoo. A clear morning had rifled through night to bring day, but the canal retained something of the darkness, a memory of the many crimes committed under and away from the collective eyeline. Few risked coming here this early, one reason it had been chosen. Frank was in his jogging gear.

"You've taken up running."

"Yes, Mr Wright. I remember you once told me you ran because one day you might need to. Well, I guess we are at that 'one day', aren't we."

Okello's speech rhythms had become normal now too, as had his movements the last time we'd met on Primrose Hill. There, he'd given me the crushing news of my likely extinction and I was wary of what forecasts he might offer next.

"Yes, we are." I exhaled dejectedly. "What have you got for us, Frank?"

He became as serious as a doctor checking the lung function of an emphysemic.

"Someone is definitely onto me. They are trying to track me online and out here."

"Can you find out where they are? Maybe we can get to them first?"

"Hmm. Possible. Next, Zokoff Holdings." Frank saw I hadn't encountered it before.

"The company's domicile is unclear but there's possibly a UK correspondence address at some kind of legal firm in Cockfosters of all places. It appears to be linked to the land in Ghana, but I haven't discovered how. Whoever set it up really doesn't want anyone to know it exists and that's why it must be important."

"Fine."

Frank frowned as he looked at me.

"Are you alright, Mr Wright? What happened in Ghana? I saw the film you sent."

"One of Royal Africa's slave mines went up in smoke two nights ago."

Frank stared at scum floating on the water that had gotten stuck in the algae thriving just beneath the surface. He was trying to figure out what he'd just heard and eventually came to the one clear conclusion that could be extracted.

"It sounds like a war."

"A very old one, and we don't win."

With that acknowledgment, I felt the weight of a thousand years trampling me down towards the relief of an oblivion that would be my only reward for stupidly challenging things the way they were.

"We need anything you can give us, Frank. I wish it wasn't the case, but I can't see anywhere to go now but forwards. If we don't, we end up like Asante and Michaels. Where does John Viner live?"

"He has a few places dotted around the world. There's an apartment off of New Bond Street."

"Banque de Montagne's office is around there."

"Yes, it's on the top floor of the building. There are fire stairs, which might give access, but the building falls under commercial regulations so night security should have a key in case of emergencies."

"Bet he's got some serious security up there."

"You'd be surprised, Mr Wright. Powerful people sometimes feel themselves invincible. It wasn't so easy to find out that the place existed at all."

Thirty metres to the west, a bicycle was rocking towards us along the uneven pathway bordering the canal. We both sucked in the air, readying ourselves as it drew parallel, then squeaked forward on its way.

"I'll take care of those two things then, Frank."

He was about to get up when I coughed.

"Frank, you've changed. Still taking the meds?"

He offered a parental smile.

"I suspect they were really not helping me, Mr Wright. Some of the thoughts I was having before – those that the British doctors called delusional and paranoid when I was in hospital – well, they turned out to be true. Royal Africa Holdings is as real today as the slave forts on West Africa's coastline."

I watched him jog away, strong as a piece of oak timber, then picked up my traveling bag to walk towards Hackney under the partial cover of the canal's camera-less banks and bridges.

The rear of the housing estate where Asante had lived was even more neglected than the front. Its overflowing large bins and untended grass formed a natural habitat for several species of vermin. I spent some time watching at a distance, because this is where I'd sit waiting for me. There was nobody save the small animals playing out their Darwinian scripts, so I took the long route round, to observe the large building's unwelcoming entrance from the vantage point of a bus stop. Double-deckers laboured by, depositing those for whom the prospect of working one standard day job was only a pipe dream.

After about an hour, it felt safe enough to run the stairs and unlock Asante's door. I was looking for something, a detail missed the first time, hidden in a false cupboard, under a floorboard or sewn into the lining of the only other jacket that hung on the rail in Asante's bedroom. The police chief-cum-security guard had used his charisma to befriend then turn one of R.A. Capital's lawyers. Then he'd tried to make himself rich off of the guy's back and had gotten them both killed. There was far more to him than suggested by the emptiness of my previous visit.

Ashley was leaning against the sofa in Asante's living room. His throat had been sliced, blood congealing on his T-shirt and down the dirty piss-stained tracksuit trousers. The head sagged forwards at an unnatural angle, giving the impression of an act of dying prayer, a final acceptance of all the unfairness inflicted upon this short life.

I gave an outward cry of panic but then reeled it back in with the next gasping breath as survival moved to assume the role of the only thing that mattered. Aside from the acid flavour of stale urine, the body didn't yet smell strongly so Ashley's death had taken place quite recently. There was no mobile phone on him. I looked closer at the corpse – his right hand had been injured in the fight. A knife sat on Asante's kitchen table, silently proclaiming its achievement. I used a plastic bag to wrap and usher the killer's weapon into my leather holdall. It would be harder to pin this one on me without a murder weapon at the scene. There was no need to stay any longer – it was time to get far away from the dead boy, from the men who did this, from suspicious neighbours and a possible life sentence for murder.

"**H**ey, Kobi."

"Bro – where've you been?" He was trying to sound irritated because it might give him some advantage.

"Where to start. You not gonna believe this, but I was in Accra for two days – just back this morning."

"Accra. Jeez, why didn't you hook me up, Jolene – I haven't been back there for fifteen years?"

If it existed at all, the thin layer of Kobi's emotional make-up somehow required him to love the country that was the source of all his pain and consequently hate everything else that supposedly kept him from returning to it. It was risky to tell him the truth that I'd been there but far riskier still not to.

"I didn't go for a holiday. There was trouble all over it, my friend. And I think the trouble's followed me back – feel like someone's watching me, some of the time at least."

Kobi didn't even pretend to care if I lived or died, but as I laid out the key facts of the R.A. Capital situation, he became more and more fascinated.

"The main funders of transatlantic slavery? Phew, Jolene, that puts us right in the belly of the beast."

Kobi's 'us' felt like the sound of music to a person who'd been deaf since birth.

Mona's Beauty and Massage served a loyal local clientele from a mid-sized unit on one of Cockfosters' main shopping parades. Mona, the young woman who owned it, had fashioned herself into a walking advert for the services her business offered. I popped my head across her open threshold.

"Hi, I need some beauty help this morning – any suggestions?"

She looked up from the laptop at reception and made a quick decision to go the 'liking me' route.

"How about a massage instead? Wednesday's always a quiet day so we have space."

"Oh, just off a plane this morning – that would be pretty great. Do you have somewhere I could freshen up – haven't had a chance to get home yet?"

"Where'd you go?"

"Accra."

"Oh, my dad's hometown! We have a shower room in the back, umm…"

"Joseph – my friends call me Jo."

I paid for a forty-five-minute head stroke and neck rub. Mona had the masseuse set me down face forwards in a vertical chair. When I woke up, her glittering eyelashes were blinking at me with some concern.

"You were moaning as you slept – kept saying the name Michael."

It was embarrassing to have spread the detritus of my recent past out on display for two people I didn't even know.

"Yeah, I've been under some stress the last couple of weeks. A successful black businesswoman probably knows what that word 'stress' really means."

"Phew, don't I!" I was still that mystery that needed unravelling. "You from Ghana – your parents, I mean?"

"My dad's Nigerian, so that's not why I went there."

"Why then?"

A quality in Mona meant I couldn't lie to her. It was a familiarity, or just a promise of care, that circumvented my usual pathways of cunning.

"I'm a private investigator chasing up a case. Can't say much other than it brought me here."

She tapped long sparkling finger nails on the narrow table of her greeting desk.

"Here?"

I nodded.

"There's a lawyer's office that I need to visit – that's before you offered me the massage, of course, which really is great by the way!"

"Oh, them upstairs. They're barely ever there. I sometimes wonder why they rent it all because the money isn't nothing, you know. If he comes, it's only ever on Fridays."

The masseuse finished trying to extract the traumas stored in my neck and shoulders. I was plenty grateful for the effort and showed it with my tip.

"Mona, when this case is over, maybe I can come back and we talk some more. I would love to hear your story." The light in her eyes felt warm, like something to try and stay alive for.

"Soon then – thanks for the shower."

The office of Ayers, Cranborne and Partners had no front door onto the parade's footfall. They didn't want the business that Cockfosters might provide. To get to the room above Mona's, you walked round to the unkept backside of the terrace of shops. Old bits of office furniture rested uselessly alongside decades of ignored surplus stock, like some informal land dump for failed entrepreneurship. Innocuity was the place's main defence. Nobody who mattered would ever guess it was there.

I broke in through a boarded-up window at basement level and made a way up felt-carpeted stairs that had absorbed decades of tobacco smoke. The peeling veneer of the office door would probably have eventually given to a foot but picking its double locks was far quieter. If solicitors ever worked here, they were from a different era. The one-roomed office was not blessed with a phone nor any computer. In the far corner, across from dirt-filled window panes, sat five grey metal chests of drawers in which were meticulously labelled the details of hundreds of companies using this address as their own. Zokoff's file was easy to locate near the back of the last cabinet. The date of the company's registration put the whole thing at less than a month old. The names of the company's owners had been deliberately redacted but there, stamped boldly across several pages, was a picture that revealed everything I needed to know.

Outside, the summer sun shouted from the joy of a knowledge that we now both held. It was the secret of how to inject life into things that would otherwise be forever dead. By the time I got back to the Rye from the featureless north London suburb, that joyful sun was still hot but starting to consider how it might adjourn for the afternoon to the safety of a careful dusk.

The membrane of caution that had pressed against every moment since I'd found Ashley dead now fit less tautly. Kobi was watching those who would watch me from the back of an old white van he'd acquired and parked in one of the spaces that littered the foot of my tower block.

The gun remained unmolested in its place by the kitchen – nobody had been here, which was surprising given they'd have tortured Ashley before cutting his throat.

I let a sweet sting of alcohol release every cell in my body from the curse of the bad that they'd both seen and done. My mind expanded with this process, making accelerating connections like streams of interspersing fireworks against the blackest of nights.

The real question was, who were the 'they' that had finished Ashley's short experience in this world? R.A. Capital's killers didn't need to take the risk of torturing a poor kid in a thin-walled council flat where anyone might call the police, but then *they likely were* the police; the courts and prisons too, if need be. Could it have been that Ashley resisted? That as death approached, he'd uncovered a bravery that had been beaten out of him early on? That might have necessitated an onsite execution. But the knife on the table didn't fit. Why leave it for someone to find? Then maybe it was only for me to find so that I'd know what had and would happen – and that they didn't care about getting caught: a deliberate display of power intended to terrorise the next target.

After a couple of tumblers filled to the brim, I dropped to sleep in the balcony chair and my soul was truly thankful for that time away.

24

WEDNESDAY EVENING

The screams came from below. A sharp smack slapped me into more wakefulness, sounding like a thin steak hitting the butcher's board. Then an anguished cry, more screaming, a dull thud, another, and some whimpering from Mr Forster downstairs after he'd been hit with something hard by his wife.

I pointed my weary frame towards the safety of the bathroom, the place I'd always hidden as a child when the arguments got too much. Splashes of ancient scenes from an ageing projector flashed into awareness: two people who'd for a while called themselves my parents. Showering by instinct, my mind edged back to balancing the constants and variables that described the equation of survival.

The drab security guard uniform donated by Everett was two sizes big: baggy enough to easily conceal a small gun strapped tightly under an armpit. Kobi seemed to be enjoying the spectacle of my life being in peril, nodding faintly in comedic solemnity as I lumbered by his van with the reluctance of an animal headed to the exsanguination pen.

A number twelve bus rocked purposefully through London's early rush hour traffic, taking me towards an uncertainty that, until now, I'd been trying to avoid. But the knowledge I'd earned and the urgency brought about by Ashley's death dragged me to the last place and one last chance to make it. How could anyone persuade Frank Okello's inflictor of so many oppressions, just maybe, just once, to leave these victims alone?

The night security guard at the Banque de Montagne office in Mayfair had suddenly been called away to a family emergency this evening and Everett's people had then ensured that Chris Brown fitted the required profile.

At 7pm on the dot, the ageing Ghanaian day incumbent, Nathaniel, handed me an instruction booklet and a list of assigned tasks for the evening, one of which was to regularly check the lift up to the top floor. He was too tired to be suspicious. Everett had once told me that London's economy operated on the basis that people like Nathaniel worked twice the hours for half the wage they should be earning, and it didn't seem to matter if that meant they had little chance of doing a proper job.

Although it wasn't named in the wall panel of floor numbers, the top level was accessed directly by the building's main lift with a special key that, when inserted below the alarm bell sign, took you all the way up to a single door. Beyond this, there was a simple lock for which I also had the key, overseen by cameras feeding down to my security station on the ground floor. Frank Okello had guessed right. The entire set-up relied far too heavily on a security guard sat behind the building's impenetrable front doors. At 10pm, I disabled the alarm and crept in.

Robert Viner's apartment occupied the entire footprint of the top of the Banque de Montagne office building. A short wide hallway led directly into a room twenty-five metres in length and fifteen wide. The whole piece was subtly lit by thin beams emanating from hidden strips along floors and ceilings, which gave the impression that the room was somehow floating at the hand of some alien anti-gravity technology. The place was as clean as an operating theatre. Poured cream concrete flooring offered little sanctuary for dirt and long white walls carried no shelving for dust to rest alongside fond memories. I drifted quickly forward, watching myself as if from the outside, wondering somewhere if it was the closeness of death that did it.

The kitchen, positioned behind a large white island at the end of the palatial first room, was similarly bare. Utensils and appliances lurked stealthily behind opaque glass cupboards waiting in eerie calm to be drafted into action. Along the length of wall opposite ran a continuous window that looked out across Mayfair towards the trees of Hyde Park. I forced a smile at the company the view kept with my meagre balcony at home. Their shared purpose somehow brought me closer to the man whose life I was now violating to save my own.

Furthest from where I had entered, two rooms led off the main space. One was Viner's sleeping quarters, which was bare of anything except a low, wide bed in the Japanese style. Cupboards were merged with white walls, framed again by the subtlest of shadow lighting. He didn't live here much. The few carefully arranged clothes within offered me little encouragement.

The second room only managed to hint at being an office. It was staffed by a rectangular concrete desk without drawers, a recliner in the Danish modernist style and no computer terminal. I sat down in the chair, lacking any idea what to do next. There was so little to grasp hold of here – nothing, simply nothing. Even the lighting was hidden from sight. I followed the photonic line that was somehow projected around the room. There was a piece of that pristine white wall under which the lasered journey became slightly less bright. Not greatly noticeable, but still it was there!

My breathing tapered as I swept under the desk looking for a switch of some sort. Nothing. I tapped the wall where light had been muffled. The sound returning was different than that of the wall to its side. Tracks of sweat started to scrape down my face as the tension of finding what lay behind there shot high doses of stress hormones into my system. The room was so bare. I reclaimed the seat to focus on what might be out of place in a confined space with only two objects. Not the things themselves, but perhaps how they related to the room... or... to each other? A chair and a desk; it was so simple, a desk and a chair. My mind snapped – a desk without a chair; the chair wasn't at the desk, it was pointed at the wall, which was how I'd gotten to see the thinning of the light. I pressed a flush wooden button under the right arm of the iconic piece of seating. A double door clicked and pivoted itself into an entrance.

My stomach convulsed, the taste of poisonous liquids that the body produced to shred organic matter flooding throat and nostrils. I stood up weakly like a geriatric patient shuffling to the endoscopy table.

Viner's secret room was a windowless cave where the treasure of truth came to hide. The computer terminal he used to direct his multinational empire sat on a small desk at the far end. On the walls were carefully hung trophies from soldiering days: weapons, a rusty machete, an old AK-47 and then the large stuffed heads of various animals no doubt executed in pursuit of what Viner considered pleasure.

Opposite these lay framed photos: a youthful Viner with his unit; white men at war somewhere in the world on behalf of more important ones at home. Other pictures showed a middle-aged Viner standing next to or in close conversation with some of Africa's great post-independence leaders and more pictures still of a now older version of the man with well-known political figures from the upper echelons of Europe's recent history.

In the centre of the room lay three glass boxes highlighted from below with an intense greenish light which meant you could see inside only from directly above. I moved, with the caution of forest prey, the five metres towards the centre of a dread that had consumed me ever since Frank Okello had ripped open the veil one afternoon on Newington Green.

The first box, titled *London, England, 1643*, held the dried remains of the dead black child from Samuel Pepys' diaries. Maybe ten years old, he was placed in the foetal position, his head jarred back in an unnatural posture.

I started to feel my insides collapsing like a skyscraper in the instant of demolition, just after the explosion and before the free fall of cement, brick and steel. The second larger box, *Green Park Plantation, Jamaica, 1791*, held similarly treated remains, this time of a naked black teenage girl. Her skeleton had been arranged in the posture of a quadruped, her neck and head twisted in a visceral parody of wildness. The last box had to be larger, as it contained the body of a fully grown man. The corpse lay on his back with chains from a piece of floor attached to his wrists and ankles. An agonised cry had been arranged on the lovingly preserved features to capture the moment before his life ended. As with the others, a plaque on the box proclaimed place and time of death, *Port-au-Prince, Haiti, 2004*.

There had been many instances of fear before this. I had learnt how to navigate these through techniques of breathing and grounding in the reality of the present. But the vacuum of panic that consumed me in the moment ran to depths that the training couldn't reach, across generations past and into futures that hadn't yet unfolded. Paralysis of the diaphragm removed my ability to stand and so I sat down, resting against the thick glass of the final exhibition cabinet, struggling like every other organism finding itself in a hostile environment to simply get to the next second, that next inhalation, caring nothing for what happened beyond a basic metabolic act. I eventually toppled rightwards, barely feeling the cold of the grey concrete against ribs and legs. From its hidden strapping, the small pistol's handle pushed up into my armpit, nudging the soft tissue occasionally, tugging at the thread of what was needed to get back.

It is hard to figure how long I laid there, merely

existing, but at some point, movement did return. I followed what little of the pitiful plan was left, making my dazed way out of the hidden room, even managed to press the wooden button inside the chair so that the wall swished shut with a finality that felt like the last sentence of an obituary.

Outside the apartment, I acted mostly instinctively, an automaton or still just some lower order of life form, straightening the uniform, checking again for the reassurance of the small metal reprieve under my arm. I made a path carefully down the fire stairs towards the reception area and the security guard's desk that I was supposed to be occupying.

25

THURSDAY MORNING

When I arrived downstairs, a heavy-set middle-aged man, dressed in a waxed cotton motorbike jacket, had occupied my seat. He had the faded cut of a military barber and was tanned in a way that made him resemble a popular professional wrestler I used to watch on television before Poorang's dances rose to hold sway over my inner realm of violence. I looked briefly across at his company of two, advancing quickly towards their victim, and made a choice. There was only one chance now and it was neither to fight nor to run.

"Excuse me, what are you doing here, how did you get in? I can call the police, you know!"

The wrestler shook his head and sneered as if listening to a bad joke, tapping my desk rhythmically with the thick digits of his large paws. He didn't have to believe me yet, but I needed to introduce doubt, a tiny cordial of sweet complacency in his bitter liquid of bad intentions. It was really my only shot; the seed of the idea that I was like Yaw Asante, just another brown nobody who'd stumbled onto my pointless death as accidentally as I had my insignificant life. Most men like this underestimated people like me, and I needed him to revert swiftly to that happy median.

I waited a second so that the choreography would gel, walked towards the desk as if about to grab the phone, then felt the anticipated hand on my shoulder. Ordinarily, that would have been a signal for me to duck, swivel and transfer my weight in some way, but now I allowed the heavy brute on my right to stop, then yank me away like a rag doll, stumbling backwards over his size-fourteen boot and falling to the ground. I made a performance of looking ruffled and frightened and accentuated the West African notes in my accent to add to the effect I needed to have on them.

"L… look, what is going on? I am the night security here – that's all. I don't get paid for trouble. Take what you want – anything! I won't stop you. I have the keys to the offices and… and… and there's a huge apartment up on the top. Maybe some valuables in there!"

The reception's phone rang and the wrestler picked up to receive instruction, replying economically with a cockney twang to questions he was being asked by his commanding officer.

"No, he's not… probably just fancied a peek inside. Yep. OK, we'll bring him with us."

I got up quickly, widened my eyes to show terror.

"Bring me in? Where? Listen, this is not fair – I have not done anything!"

The third assailant, a short muscular man who'd made up for the deficits of genetics with a life of gym effort, punched me in the gut and I doubled over, falling theatrically onto the marble reception flooring, allowing spittle to stain my face and uniform.

The wrestler surveyed me with a bored contempt he might have used for a troublesome fly.

"Got into the flat upstairs eh, boy?"

It felt good to hear him call me 'boy'. I was rapidly moving to zero in his hierarchy of threat; just some stupid black fool who wanted to see how the important people lived.

"I… I just wanted to have a look inside. I tried all the keys and pushed on the door – that's it. Who lives there?"

"Give us those keys."

I dutifully handed them to the squat gym addict.

The three mercenaries led me out of the front door into Mayfair's midnight. I thought about Yaw Asante and how easy it was for truly evil people to terrify the nearly innocent into total compliance. Once inside the car, a rough sack was thrust over my head and the 'shortie' pushed me sideways and down into the plush comfort of leather upholstery. There was less legroom in the back, so it had to be him. He kept a threatening hand on my side to feel any impulse I might develop for escape. From within the bag, I whimpered, shook and cried every so often for effect.

We headed east for about ten minutes – no traffic at all at the time, five miles at most. The car's tyres were met with the soothing texture of hard cobble, then stopped abruptly as if they'd had their fill of it. As I was forced out of the vehicle, I feigned limpness, begging, moaning and crying for God, my mother and Jesus the father. The air here carried a faint flavour that I recognised.

They led me down some stairs into a basement, turned right after fifteen paces, then left. A heavy door opened and I was thrown into a windowless dark cell adorned with stone for walls and floor. I found the corner to the left of the door, wedged myself into it and waited. I thought about the pathetic woman I had for a mother who'd been strapped into rooms this size at times when she'd become uncontrollable. What might that have done to her already compromised psyche?

After some more time, which could have been hours, I heard boot steps crunching ominously on the basement floor. I rose swiftly and stood by the side of the door. When it opened, the wrestler didn't even have time to be confused as the bullet released by the mechanism of my gun macerated the part of his brain that met the temple. The soldier with the large boots committed the fatal mistake of backing off, was shot twice in the belly, and as he then lurched forward, desperate to make it stop, I stepped away, shooting him in the back of the head before he'd smashed into the floor. Survival thickens focus and I moved at speed, turning right, fifteen paces left, then out of the basement and up wrought-iron stairs to ground level.

The tang in the air came from Brick Lane's many Bengali eateries. That familiarity offered a degree of solace as the protective part of me focused itself on the next point in my dilemma. There were two dead soldiers, but more would soon be searching. I needed shelter. Royal Africa's dungeons had probably lived here for centuries, close enough to but just far enough away from the City of London where the whole enterprise had been conceived. This was the heartland of a power that had captured entire parts of the world's history for its own profit.

Keeping away from the penumbra between buildings, I tried to will myself into shadow form, dashing through Whites Row, across Commercial Road into Fashion Street, which fed directly onto Brick Lane. My shadow fled past Yiolanda's boutique, desperate for an unlikely light inside that might signify she'd stayed back for some reason, to balance the books or sift through old stock. There was nothing to see there.

With that disappointment came a terror that delivered its own effects. Windows of old buildings, mutated into large knowing eyes yearning to trap the runaway for their master, offering no sanctuary by way of broken panes or loosened closures. Eventually, all I could do was hunker into the doorway of a Balti Curry House, spotting to the north, in the light of the bagel shop that inexplicably stayed open twenty-four hours a day, the outlines of figures coordinating their search, then running off. There would be some to the south too, more threatening still for the fact that I hadn't seen them. My eyes rolled upwards in supplication to whatever God had moulded the reality of this wretched existence and, as they did so, spotted something. It was there across the narrow road: the sign of the Golden Arch Tandoori House and a grey door next to it where Beryl, the late Wade Barker's favourite prostitute, was probably working right now. Delores, of all people, had given me a chance!

I scrambled across the road, hammering the buzzer until someone answered.

"Hello." It was a voice accustomed to all manner of deviance that the human spirit might concoct.

"You don't have an appointment and I am busy at the moment. The door you are standing at is made of solid steel."

There was no choice but to not believe her.

"Listen, Beryl, isn't it? Delores Machado, you know her. She gave me your details – said if ever I was feeling… you know, in need, I might be able to come here to see you. You know her, right?"

With the intercom silence arrived my last rites. A final plan quickly began to formulate from these ruins: to make a run for it down the narrow Hanbury Street and over to the park where I'd first offered to meet Wade Barker. That plan hadn't strayed anywhere near the envisaged outcome. Neither would this, but I was fast and had some bullets left if they got close enough. I readied myself to make the first dash, then the door opened and a pretty, petite woman gave me the sort of smile that told me my money was wanted here after all.

The door closed like a sigh of safety and I followed her upstairs, watching a motion of her buttocks that was intended to encourage me to part with my cash. I thought about how this was my second brothel stay in only a few days and what that implied about the life which I'd built from the rubble of childhood.

There was a landing before we entered the room where Beryl took payment with eyes, which hardened fast as she said the words.

"It's a hundred and fifty an hour and extra for anything special."

After we'd crossed into the unusually pleasant bedroom, I lay back, fully clothed, on the California king while my host tried to work out what was going on with this one.

"Beryl, can you tell me the time? My mobile got broken earlier and I don't have a watch on."

She didn't really believe me but pointed at the clock on the chaise longue that sat between the bed and a view east across the dirty backs of shops.

"It's 2:15am, darlin'. You look tired – you wanna shower or something?"

A large ensuite bathroom fed off the bedroom's beiges and whites.

"You live here."

"How'd you guess?"

"It's nice – well looked after."

I was surprised to find myself wandering. She looked at my erection.

"Time for a shower?"

I left the uniform and the gun in the bathroom, returning with a towel only.

"I recognise you, you know. You're Delores's ex. She showed me a picture of you both a few years ago. It was a happy one. I think she must have really liked you back then."

My eyes flitted from hers, ashamed of what I wanted now and how I'd lied to gain access to it. This was the sort of man I'd become. But the greatest thing about the many prostitutes I had met in my life was that they pretended not to judge the poor shells of men who crawled to them. She grabbed my towel away and I paid her for another hour after the first was done.

26

THURSDAY MORNING

"Kobi, it's me. Please call this number."

I'd jogged up Kingsland Road away from the City of London at about 8am and bought some more phones from a seller who kept a stall around the edge of Dalston Market. It had taken two hundred pounds more to persuade Beryl to let me stay a few hours. Her business was done for the night but she kept another equally well-appointed dwelling below the bedroom, which served as a living area. I embraced the couch as if I'd been on a starvation course in dreaming.

While running, I juggled images, facts and feelings from the night before, trying to arrange them into some form of coherence that would speak sense to me.

None of the killers I'd encountered had drawn knives and none knew who I was or even that there was a possibility of a me. They'd not killed and tortured Ashley, although that didn't mean some of their colleagues hadn't and reported back separately to headquarters. I quickly found myself in London Fields, a dream of a park that attempted to bridge the cosseted aspirations of those living in some of the expensive housing stock on its fringes with the more immediate concerns of the people who found themselves in the many council estates that were situated nearby. I sat on a bench opposite some quiet tennis courts, watching the odd finance worker commuting towards their daily sharing-out of the pie, wondering how these two realties had managed to coexist in one park and one city for so long. The pressure of loneliness weighed on me like a hundred metres of ocean overhead. There was no safety at home and no friends to help except for a psychopath who would not waste a second grieving if my existence came to an end. I called Yiolanda and got voicemail.

"Hey, it's Jo. I just wanted to say that… that you've always been… since school I've always liked you, looked up to you and even loved you. If I get through what I'm currently on, I want you to know that. I don't have anyone. There's no one who cares if I live or die and the second is looking much more likely at the moment, so I called you because I needed someone to know and it was you."

I almost inhaled the full English breakfast at a worker's café round the side of Kingsland Shopping Centre. A local history I'd once read told me 'King's

Land', had been built near the site of an old leper hospital established in the thirteenth century by the merchants of the City of London to keep the terrible disease at bay. The flavour of the salty cured meat and oiled bread gifted an uncommon level of comfort, which led my mind back to the few paths left to discover what had happen to my friend, Ashley. I purchased some black jeans and unmarked trainers, a T-shirt, a dark-blue hooded jumper and baseball cap from a couple of shops now open on the high street and then made the first dangerous call of the day.

"Joseph." There was no hint of apprehension in his voice, although he had little reason for that sitting in his South London fortress.

"Cushnie. Would like to buy some more refills for the glue gun."

"I see."

"Job's still going."

"Come round."

He put the phone down and that was it – he didn't have to say anymore because when a man like him told you to come round, he meant right now.

I was inside Cushnie's bunker within the hour, handing Nick the pistol. The scarred man took the weapon and aimed the barrel at my chest, smiling menacingly. But we both knew today wasn't the day he was going to do that. I found the kingpin in his room eating papaya for breakfast.

"Didn't know you were a health-food man."

He sliced his eyes quickly up at my attempt at humour but let it slide.

"It's good to keep the system clean. Allows the brain to work faster."

There was no sign of Lisa today. He didn't gesture for me to sit.

"Tell me, what are you doing on this one, Joseph?" Cushnie wanted to see what assets could be realised from my situation but also if simply knowing me created any potential liability.

"The hooligans have been dealt with. They don't even know we exist."

I used the 'we' so that he would know Kobi was involved. Cushnie would easily take on both of us if needed but that name alone added a significant factor to the accounting he ran to decide whether to act or not.

"I've had the feeling that I was being followed since yesterday afternoon. Don't know who it is yet."

Cushnie looked intently at the large bowl of fruit he was consuming, vetting pieces for size, juice and potential sweetness.

"That was me. You disappeared for a couple of days and I got the idea you were doing something stupid so I put a couple of my boys on you – ones you didn't know. They got a call you were in Hackney."

"But I told Ashley where I was going – he still working for you on the fringes, right?"

Either the man was a master poker player or he didn't know anything about my dead friend.

"That addict? Threw his useless arse out a year ago before I had to finish him myself!"

"Well, if it was you having me followed, I'll probably only need a clip – still jumpy as hell."

Cushnie leapt deftly onto the opportunity to make some more money.

"You don't need a gun, Joseph. Who are you, Clint Eastwood? Get caught with that shit, it's five years inside minimum, and then maybe I've got to sort you out just in case you give me up."

I held his granite gaze for as long as it took to convince him I wasn't giving in easily. As usual, his laser-sharp reasoning was hard to counter even if I had wanted to risk the danger of doing so.

"So this has been a kind of deposit and lease agreement?"

He laughed out loud, spitting fragments of papaya onto the table.

"I like you, Joseph. You're quick and somehow you know shit too. Let's say I just loaned it to you for the week at a very high rate of interest."

The session was over. I hadn't really come for bullets anyway. On the way out, Cushnie asked me as if I really did work for him.

"Can you ask Carl to come in when you see him?"

I walked down the hallway wondering whether Lisa was at the shops or in a shallow grave somewhere. Carl saw me out. He was less heavily muscled than his fellow pit bull, Nick; closer in physique and spirit to their owner.

"Hey, Carl. Ashley tells me you and him used to be good mates."

Carl stopped at the fortified door, showing me the way out with a flick of his head.

"That cunt Ashley? Fuck off, Joseph!"

27

THURSDAY AFTERNOON

A jubilant waft of the South East London air met my lungs, jogging away from the dirty corner where Cushnie's bunker sat in wait like some ancient concrete predator. I was moving, thinking and feeling but still mostly a dead person waiting for the fact to catch up. The jewel of an idea had formed about Ashley's murder, but before I could get to it, there loomed the sort of mountains ahead that even the most extreme climbers would pass on.

I left another message for Kobi, then switched phones. The train from Penge got me into Victoria in twenty minutes – a short hop to Mayfair and the Banque de Montagne office. The prim receptionist didn't remember me, which hurt a little.

"Hi, I'm here to see Flo Danjuma, please."

"Of course… Mr?"

"Wright, Joseph Wright."

"You're not in the diary, Mr Wright."

"Please ring up. Tell him it's about the gold mines in Ghana. He'll want to meet."

The leather-upholstered seat of the marble vestibule was identical to the one in Viner's study and sat directly opposite the receptionist's array of cameras. The polished floor onto which I had been thrown only a few hours before had been well cleaned, shining back at me in immaculate denial.

After ten minutes, Danjuma materialised outside the lift, dressed in a beautiful soft-cut black linen blazer and trousers. He looked tense. The Nigerian had never seen me before, but I felt like we were old friends.

"Mr... Wright, is it?"

"Yes – and you are Folusha Danjuma." It gave me a cool pleasure to watch my familiarity raise his well-manicured discomfort several notches.

"Viner want to see me?"

The mention of the name made him more wired still. We elevated in silence and, reaching the apartment, which had no name, he pointed me towards the front door I'd breached in the early hours of the morning.

"You not invited, Flo?"

He sniffed and pressed the lift door shut.

Robert Viner opened, smiling pleasantly as if welcoming a new client to the R.A. Capital fold. He was far smaller than I had imagined, a white man of maybe sixty, delicate sun-weathered features crowned by tufts of thinning blond hair. The most unusual thing about him was how physically fit he looked; there was no hint of fat under the gleaming white cotton shirt, belted with a leather wreath at the waist, over soft light-blue slim-cut trousers. Here was a man on permanent holiday who'd probably never missed a day of work in his adult life.

Viner led me into the minimalist living room and stopped at the vast window, looking out over the wealthiest square kilometres on the planet. The discipline of a former military existence was infused into every movement. Even at his age, he was still very capable of both giving and receiving high levels of violence.

He talked to the window and almost to himself, as if I was barely worthy of attention. His tone was still affable, belying the subject matter it was exploring: the issue of my existence in his world. He had little reason not to be pleasant – his life would go on regardless of my fate, but there was always the question of whether the real John Viner would show up here.

"The men didn't follow basic training last night." He was annoyed with the two dead corporals for how they'd expired in his service.

"They were unable to adjust. Some people find that difficult."

"Because you are black, you mean? Yes, stupid white men make that mistake a lot with you, I imagine, but I'd bet it's not very often they pay for it with their lives."

It felt strangely exhilarating to be having this conversation with the monster of my nightmares. The Grim Reaper offered knowledge for a life on this earth, but was that ever truly a good deal?

"It's an unusual situation all round."

"I've known some of your greatest people, Joseph, known them well. They were mostly in over their heads."

"If you understood where I grew up, you would see those aren't my people."

"Your people, Africans; whatever we might call them. They were always totally outmatched and most knew it."

I inhaled as heavily as if I was making the oxygen I breathed and gathered up my flimsy will into some form of intention. It was time to push, to exorcise the puss sitting at Viner's core – that thing that had him keep dried black people as trophies. Only with this demon could any deals be made.

"Speaking of being in over your head, have those great African mates of yours heard about your land title problems in Ghana? Those mines must be really profitable with all that free labour."

He twisted quickly away from the beautiful scenery to regard me with unfeeling grey eyes. Here was a smallish ageing white man, totally unafraid of what I might do to him, utterly lacking in fear or guilt or maybe any emotion at all.

"Do you know, Joseph, that we've existed for

quite a while in one form or another? I am merely the custodian of a history, you understand. A history of…"

"European conquest."

"People like you might call it that but really it's… it's… human advancement."

"I am not sure the humans working in your mines would see it that way."

He smiled fondly like you would at a pet who'd just witnessed you commit murder. I could see the change coming.

"The problem with your people, Joseph – do you know what it is, what it has been since before your pitiful countries were granted independence on their route to total failure?"

The monster's voice carried a higher pitch at its edge – Viner's still but with less control.

"You aren't diligent historians. You neither understand nor appreciate the underlying nature of the forces that shape everyone's daily reality."

"I've been starting to get to grips with those recently myself. Royal Africa Capital had some interesting predecessors. Can see why you have to do things in the shadows now though – it's all a bit seventeenth century."

"We gained that land in the Gold Coast perfectly legally."

"Isn't your Gold Coast called Ghana now? Maybe there's just some newer variables that you've missed in the last fifty years."

He had seemed to ignore the correction, but it enraged him.

"But let's look what happens a few decades later. Here's a mess of a land title issue, floating in a disaster of a legal system fashioned by a country with no future." The affable face transformed with the volume of hatred it held.

"Africans. Cretinous, outdated chieftaincy systems. Can you really believe any of you will win against nation states, corporations, pools of wealth that date back to the Crusades?"

"I don't know. Isn't one lesson of history that things can change…"

"Seriously. Just look at you now!" The higher pitch interrupted, annoyed that it had chosen to explain anything at all to one of the ants it crushed on a daily basis.

"Look at your people: poverty-ridden, illiterate, utterly irrelevant!"

He stopped for me to absorb the racist rhetoric.

"As far as I can see, Britain has its own version of chieftaincy sitting right over there."

I gestured towards the large palace south of Hyde Park. He understood and instantly tired of debate.

"I work with partners, Joseph. If you could actually fathom who they were, you wouldn't be with us very long."

"Staying alive is why I am here. I figure you don't know where those land titles for your mines have gone."

Viner raised an eyebrow in sarcastic anticipation. "And you do?"

"I might be able to find out in return for…"

He'd stopped listening to me bargain for my life and was ordering pros and cons on the balance sheet of his world view.

"Why should I believe you have the ability to find them?"

"Because I got to you here. Because I knew enough to try and save myself. Because I've seen that den of horrors back there behind the pure white wall of your office."

A muscle in his cheek spasmed involuntarily.

"And why do you believe we will let you live after we get what we need?"

"Actually, I've got no choice other than to believe it, but you know that. Plus, I might just be more useful to you alive than dead. Then there's the film I've recently made. It's a kind of travel diary taking in the wonderful world of Royal African Capital. It starts in a Ghanaian slave mine and ends up here in this apartment actually, behind that wall in your office. You might think you can get to the people I have that will put that shit all over the internet, but you probably already suspect how good they are. You might even believe you could manage the fallout given your contacts. But tell me. Is it really worth the risk for you: all that palaver, when all we want is to just stay breathing and be left alone?"

Two pale-grey pools of malevolent consciousness

looked up at me for a long moment, giving no indication through empathy or anger whether I'd be alive later tonight.

"Bring me the land titles. You can see your way out."

With that, the lunatic returned to surveying all the human insects crawling about below on the streets of Mayfair.

Danjuma was waiting down at reception.

"Hey, Flo."

He ignored my over-familiar tone.

"How about we meet at your mews house at 5pm?"

The bald-headed intermediary nodded imperceptibly and let me on my way.

28

THURSDAY AFTERNOON

The sun was shining brightly on the fashionable district of Shoreditch where some of London's creative industries rubbed shoulders uncomfortably with those engaged in the more prosaic undertakings of global financial markets.

My body had become numb leaving the Banque de Montagne offices but was slowly regaining some feeling on the long trip. I was a modern-day Lazarus revived not by God, but by a servant of Satan, to once again experience all the sorrows and injustices that any future would offer.

The housing estate where Yaw Asante had seen out his last decades looked a touch better under the cleansing blue sheen of a perfect day in July.

I knocked on the door next to Asante's. Castle was in.

"Oh you! Mr?"

"Graves, Mr Castle. Joseph Graves."

His eyes bulged with the memory of the money I'd gifted on the last visit and that promise of more.

"Come in, come in." He gestured for me to enter the foul dwelling, but I hesitated at the door a bit longer.

"I came to tell you we've found Asante's estranged wife, who nonetheless has keys to the flat and has asked me to rescue some of her effects. As you were so helpful last time, I wondered if you might accompany me in there to aid with the search for her belongings."

The grey man's irises inflated in terror at the thought. He was simply unable to keep himself together enough to lie.

"N... no, no, no. I've got an appointment in a few minutes, so, sorry, can't help ya!"

"OK, understood. Why don't I come in for a second then. I've got a couple of questions that I am sure you can help with." The defecating mongrel wagged its tail at its returning benefactor, and I made the short unpleasant journey down the hallway, which had been refreshed since the last time with more evidence of the animal's toiletry habits.

Once in the dark living room, Castle's sagging face looked eagerly at me as I considered what cocktail of life had made him this way.

"In connection with Asante's disappearance, we have also been tasked to look for a young man, mixed-race, five foot eleven, who's been hanging round here quite a lot recently. Have you seen him?"

The crazy stick man's eyes darted suspiciously but were instantly calmed by the thought of cash.

"There's, uh… a similar reward now been placed for any information about him."

"Oh I see!"

His emaciated body relaxed an inch and he put fingers out against the cigarette-stained wallpaper to balance playfully on one scrawny leg.

"Well yeah, I have seen a young bloke as it happens: torn, dirty jacket, hangs about looking up here a lot. Mixed-race, you say? He could've been, although always hard to tell with that lot. They all look like blacks to me."

Castle didn't own a mirror and he also seemed to have totally overlooked who was sitting on his couch.

"We think he had a drug habit, unfortunately, and may have broken into Asante's flat to shoot up or smoke something. You know how they do."

The man nodded vigorously, parading the sparse rank of incisors that remained reluctantly lodged in his gums.

"Yeah, yeah, wouldn't surprise me. You know I even found the front door open one day – could easily have been 'im inside."

"I see. I guess then… it wouldn't take much for someone to have followed him in and, umm… if the lad was out of it on something… to have tried to see if he had any money on him or a mobile phone maybe? Things might easily have gotten out of control from there if he'd then woken up."

Castle's withered figure tensed rigidly, fingers clenched in seizure, as if his body had become frozen in hallucinatory re-enactment of the nightmare he'd experienced only a few days earlier. The dog sensed its owner's distress and started yapping wildly. He convulsed a scrawny neck around the walls of his self-made hell, looking for some type of hiding place from the memory of that gruesome act.

I decided to give him a way out.

"That's one hypothesis anyway. Thanks for confirming a few of the facts that we needed to check."

I brought out my wallet but then put it swiftly away in honour of my school friend Ashley Adebayo. No money this time.

Castle slumped to a tattered armchair, his awareness fixed on something that might have been the moment he'd slit a boy's throat for only a few pounds. I left him with the excitable dog, carefully placed the murder weapon in his bath amongst the piles of rubbish, before opening the front door and calmly making my exit.

Walking away, I called the police with my third mobile phone of the day, reporting a strange smell coming from number 24 Acacia Mansions and that I'd seen him arguing with his neighbour at number 25 only a few days before. I didn't care if they followed up or not. No incarceration could be worse for Castle than the one he was already experiencing. I'd met the man responsible for how Ashley ended up at the Church of The Holy Spirit Revealed and he wasn't named Castle.

The London afternoon sizzled confidently on a gleaming path towards its losing battle with night and I rode a wave of new possibilities in a brightening sea of hope. It took me only an hour to get back to the vantage point from which I had watched Danjuma's flat a few days earlier. I landed over two hours before our appointment, wanting to check if the crooked son of a Nigerian general had invented any creative scenarios for our scheduled conversation. He arrived an hour early with help. The heavily muscled man looked like he was descended from a place where brutality had been the daily reality for as long as memories had been made. His mandate was no doubt to extract facts and then teach me a harsh lesson about knowing my proper place.

Danjuma's door opened silently and I tended to the alarm pad before it could start screaming in fright. I heard them down the hall in the living room as I moved swiftly forward, gripping my metal knuckle with the rage of an endangered species.

"What's that?"

"Dunno – you go and see."

The Balkan killer's head appeared first. It was hard but he was still human and my first blow broke his cheekbone, causing a nasty hematoma to start forming. He fell back, stunned but not unconscious, and as he tried to brace himself against the back wall of the corridor to come again, I was on him, transferring my weight into a short right hook to the same broken cheek, before exploding into a left punch to the throat that laid him down with a grunt toward unconsciousness.

Danjuma arrived in time to see me stamping on the sleeping man's thick head and neck just to make sure. The athletic young Nigerian backed away into his small living area as quickly as if he'd just witnessed the devil himself dragging a soul down to hell.

He was standing and shaking slightly when I got to the room, preparing to make a last stand if need be while anticipating the pain that the monster was clearly capable of inflicting. I moved closer just for the pleasure of watching him recoil with fear.

"Now let me see. Guess he was going to take the minutes for our meeting later."

Fear kept the young West African's eyes downcast, giving the impression of silent prayer. It reminded me of Ashley's corpse after a mentally ill human scarecrow had cut his throat.

I looked around the room.

"That your mums? Must've been difficult to leave her so young. No pics of Dad though? Guess he liked the younger girls, eh?"

My victim moved his head side to side, confused and hopeless as if cornered in the jungle by some wild famished carnivore. Out in the hall, the mess of a bouncer groaned so I went back and kicked him more until he rediscovered a version of peace.

Danjuma was sitting down on one of his crappy armchairs when I returned. The break had allowed him to gather up all the charm he had left.

"Listen, brother, I don't know what you want but I am sure we can come to something here."

"So, as I was saying. It must have been hard as a seven-year-old negro off the boat and straight into an English boarding school. Is that where you learnt that survival bullshit like calling me your brother? I'd learnt a whole load of things by the time I was seven. You might say my personality was pretty formed by then."

"Listen!" He emphasised the word as if it was all I would ever need in life. "I am not sure what you want. Just say! I can help!"

"Hmm, an offer of assistance from a drowning man. Not sure I like that one. I do like the girls in the safe though. How do you get 'em to do that stuff?"

Danjuma stopped to readjust his outer mask from one of earnest engagement to quizzical interrogator. The man should have been a newsreader.

"You've been stalking me!"

The newsreader disappeared just as abruptly as he'd arrived, fearing he'd strayed too far from the tightrope of near-term survival.

"Maybe I have. Maybe I just needed to write a story that might help to save my life. Can't say I am sure myself now."

He frowned, not yet up with my meaning, so I put more meat in the stew for him.

"You discovered what Yaw Asante was up to with Lawrence Michaels, probably at the same time Viner did."

The man's expressive handsome face was a walking, talking giveaway machine.

"You either had Toks Owusu find Opoku-Brown at the land registry and hooked him up with them or you had him secretly crash the party Opoku-Brown already had going with Asante and Michaels. The second is far more likely as you knew the Cubbins lawyer could be picked up and tortured by Viner's men and wouldn't risk him giving up your names. How am I doing, Folusha?"

He hung his head, half acting. The charming con artist still fancied he was about to strike some kind of saving deal.

"So. Asante and Michaels were the fall guys, sacrificed to Viner. While he was busy focusing on them, you hastily set up Zokoff Holdings with your best friend Toks Owusu and transferred the mines across to it, facilitated by your corrupt land registry official in Ghana, the aforementioned Kwame Opoku-Brown. Toks Owusu chose the adinkra phrase, *Bese Saka*, for Zokoff. It means 'unity and wealth'. It is stamped all over the Zokoff paperwork and worn on Owusu's wrist."

I paused to see the effect of my story on its main

protagonist. The man had unveiled another act from his repertoire, crossing legs, staring at the wall opposite as if listening intently to my every precious word. He nodded gravely from time to time as if both in self-condemnation and congratulation at my brilliance.

"Opoku-Brown had to cover his tracks and remains the biggest weakness of your plan. But then, just maybe, Owusu has people in Accra who can have him disappear if Viner is getting close. You will know when that's happening too, because you are always on those phone calls."

When Danjuma raised his head to lie some more, I punched it directly on the nose. He cried in pain, grabbing his beautiful face.

"You fucking people make me vomit. You think you own everything and that a bit of fake charm can cover up the terrible shit you do. I'm just not buying it, 'brother'."

"What then? What do you want!" He was pretending to sob now.

"I want to see what's underneath all this. Let's meet the real Folusha Danjuma, shall we? You can be sure what happens next if not." I motioned towards the hallway, whose dead silence spoke to the veracity of my threat.

When the liar looked up this time, all affected friendliness was gone, the charming rake spirited off with the multitude of other characters Danjuma employed to make others like him.

"Good," I said with a bit less threat, my dragon dissipating a touch in response to finally meeting his.

"Now talk. And look at me while you do it, so I can see when you are lying."

After a while, he rubbed his shaven head with both hands and started as uncomfortably as anyone would who'd found themselves thrown into a minefield without a map.

"I don't know. We wanted to... to do something for ourselves. Here I am working for these people, not even taking a thousandth of what they make each year."

"I can see that by the furniture."

He sneered at the slight from someone unworthy to offer it.

"When you're let in, you get to start believing you are one of them; that R.A. will allow you to win big too. But then you see what they are doing in your country and you start to doubt it. There are huge farms supplying half of West Africa with overpriced food. They pay millions to militia in Northern Nigeria to protect them. Those illiterate fucking kids earn far more than I do! Can you believe they are more valuable to Viner than I am?"

"So, you earn a lot less that than you deserve. And beyond the daily experience of almost everyone, your point is...?"

"I don't know what it is. I... we... felt that we deserved better. Our countries deserved more. It's our land and it should be owned by us."

"You'd probably enslave as many Africans as Viner does."

"I'd enslave more!"

His moment of revelation seemed to spark an eagerness to explain.

"But why not? You know my father laid it out for me before he died. He asked me who I thought built the pyramids. When I said, 'The pharaohs,' he laughed. He laughed deep and hard even though he was ill because it wasn't the pharaohs. Do you know who it really was, Joseph? It was slaves! Hundreds of thousands, maybe millions, of them. Poor people, injecting their whole pointless lives into monuments that are revered thousands of years later. And attributed to…? Their kings."

Danjuma paused in awe of a truth that seemed only to be fully revealing itself to him at this very moment.

"Surely you can see, Joseph. Poor people are poor and that's all there is to it. It's a never-ending wheel. The weak, the stupid, get screwed endlessly by the powerful and the smart and so remain weak and stupid. That's how the real story goes. I cannot change it, but I can try to make sure my grandchildren's grandchildren don't suffer the same fate. It's what people like Viner and his partners have been doing for a thousand years."

The Nigerian ended his sermon, zealous eyes fixed above my head in communion with whatever divinity would deign to tolerate such a brutal version of humanity. There was nothing left for me to do here.

I got up to leave. Flo raised his palms in protection against the coming assault.

"I'm guessing you've not been to one of those mines in Ghana or wherever else you all have 'em. If you had, you might see why what you say doesn't work. Not in the end, not for you, Flo. See, to a Viner, you and I, we are the weak and the stupid. It doesn't matter what we do. He'd rather drop a nuclear bomb on those mines than have to admit differently and let them go."

The man lying in the hallway was struggling to breathe. I stepped over his gurgling noises to leave. Behind me, Folusha Danjuma started to moan with the panic of a failing parachutist.

"Joseph. Where are you going? What are you going to do? Viner? Please not Viner! Please, Joseph!"

29

THURSDAY EVENING

I was sitting out on the balcony knocking back heavy slugs of cognac when he called. Peckham Rye looked dangerous this evening – an ominous greyish-brown hue snaked between the trees.

"Uncle Ernest."

"How are you, Joseph?"

"Oh, still alive. That's something. I was going to dial you tomorrow about our case."

"Yes, that's why I am calling, in fact. Joshua lost his job at GBC two days ago. They called it 'restructuring'."

"Ugh, sorry to hear, Uncle! What's he aiming to do now?"

"Well, he wants to get back in the markets quickly, although his mother and I feel he should take a while off, give it some thought, you know."

"Yes. There are many better paths out there for him.

Aunty Sonia and you always have JK's best interests at heart – am sure he knows that."

The man I called Uncle made uncomfortable small talk before putting the phone down on my failure to save his boy's existence in a world that simply didn't want him.

The alcohol had done the job, filing off the razor-sharp edges and a warm affection rose in their place for the man who'd tried to do so right by his family. After a while, Everett's number flashed. I didn't want to answer because I knew I'd risked getting him in big trouble with that last security guard gig. Banque de Montagne would want to know how I'd gotten the job. He was clever enough to come up with something, but I could easily imagine how unpleasant a time he might be having.

I let it ring and cast my gaze out into the advancing night. There was a small bonfire being lit somewhere on the northwestern side of the Rye. People just did crazy pointless stuff out there sometimes. Maybe they found a joy in that futility, which men like Viner and me simply couldn't understand. The tumbler took a refill and my phone searched for Yiolanda's details but went no further. She'd not replied to my last message. A proclamation of love from a man who thinks he's about to be killed was just more evidence of where any life with me would end up.

Kobi finally returned my calls.

"Jolene – you're still alive." He stated the fact, rather than the feeling of joy it might bring.

"K – where you been?"

"I saw those men taking you away and thought that was it for you. Goodbye, Joseph Wright. I've been trying to keep my distance ever since because either it was a trap or if you'd somehow escaped, which clearly you have, they'd be coming for you and then maybe anyone who knows you."

Although his voice was calm, there was more than a hint of threat in this statement. I was not worth going down for and Kobi was stalking the path of doing whatever was necessary to curtail that possibility. I felt blessed that he'd checked first before rubbing me out like a wonky question mark on a six-year-old's writing pad.

"I see, Kobi. I did a deal. Am working for them in a way, to find out who swindled the land titles."

"Easy. That's Yaw Asante and the clueless white lawyer, from what you explained earlier." Kobi had perfect recall of any conversation.

"Yes, but turns out their scam was intercepted by another group inside the R.A. Capital organisation. They are Africans – one Nigerian, one Ghanaian – public school types who were just on the make. One of them begged me yesterday not to give him up."

In the silence that followed, I imagined my friend sitting wherever he was pitying the useless sentimentality of everyday humans.

"It's fine. I know the answer, bro."

"Good. If it's you or them, there isn't even a

question to ask. Sounds like the niggahs should have known what they were getting into when they started."

The conversation was over and I reached shakily for the second bottle of the XO brandy sitting eagerly under my balcony table. I didn't get far into that one.

My father woke me on the sofa, stroking my five-year-old ears and head. He looked across at my mother, who was slim and youthful with the joy of love still in her eyes. They shared a joke about me, an anecdote they would later fondly tell friends. My mother called over from the kitchenette.

"Hey, sleepy head, it's been such a busy day – how about some supper?"

We didn't use the table because I preferred to have a picnic in the centre of the small living room. My mother cooked pancakes as Dad spread the cloth over the warm floor. When ready, she brought the large pile, revelling in my joy at the sight of them, and he poured some water in a plastic cup, carefully adding drops of my favourite blackcurrant cordial. We sat and my parents laughed, catching my hands every time I tried to sneak away yet another pancake. Then we relaxed back on the couch, watching cartoons on the television. My father read me a story before I closed my eyes to welcome a peaceful sleep.

I woke up for real this time on the same sofa, feeling

the wetness of tears on my cheeks that sprung from that deep chasm of never having.

My head and neck were washed in the cold tap. It was 5am and I felt sick with the poison that my bottled French redeemer increasingly seemed to hide so cunningly under her silk vest. My phone had Viner's number. He was up already.

"Joseph – you have something for me."

"Flo Danjuma and his best friend, John Owusu, recently created an offshore company called Zokoff Holdings, which they used to take your land once they'd found out that Asante and Lawrence Michaels were trying to do the same. I would also check out the lawyer, Taylor, only because he went to school with them, but I suspect he's not involved because he is likely British secret service."

"I see."

There was a pause in which I sensed he was almost impressed.

"We may, from time to time… have need of your advice. You seem uniquely positioned to get into certain cracks, so to speak."

"I am just like your household cockroach. If you're prepared to pay for it. I won't come cheap." In that moment, I fantasised about killing the bastard, pictured the look in his eyes when he knew he'd lost it all to someone like me. Maybe he felt it too.

"Fine, Joseph. We will see then."

Mist hovered over the Rye like a web of magic cast

by some nocturnal wizard. The spell would be gone in a couple of hours as the fantasy realm receded into memories of the dawn. I had failed to help my uncle's son, had colluded in the serial killing of a man who didn't deserve that his last experience on this earth be one of being butchered by pure evil. I'd inflicted pain on the two continents that had given birth to me. There was the betrayal of two young African men, raised to privilege but soon to taste agonising, premature deaths. And now I was on the payroll of an organisation that hated me, and everyone remotely like me. I was alive, but for what? I leaned over the balcony staring blankly at the concrete below. It was either this right now or something else…

Then, unexpectedly, that something else appeared… the memory of a girl rescued from a Ghanaian slave mine, her determined face suffering the insufferable. Suffering but carrying on regardless.

The leather holdall didn't need to live up to its name. There were so few possessions to carry away: a picture of Kate at the beginning, a soft brown belt that had belonged to my father and some silver dice given to me a long time ago by a Nigerian uncle who looked as big as a bear to the six-year-old he'd remembered at the gift shop. Some lives drew so little gravity in the universe that even the most basic material didn't seem to stick.

I fled tattered and weeping down the six flights, away from the home to which I'd been carried straight off the midwife's table, the place where two parents had, for a brief while, dared to imagine themselves to be far better than they ever were. Away from a pain that hung so heavy at times that I was certain I wouldn't be able to resist that joyful dash to the tarmac below. And away from the balcony with its view of Peckham Rye, which had nourished me through the years like an infant nestled in his mother's loving embrace.